BEWARE, THE SNOWMAN

Look for more Goosebumps books
by R.L. Stine:
(see back of book for a complete listing)

Goosebumps®

BEWARE, THE SNOWMAN

R.L. STINE

AN
APPLE
PAPERBACK

SCHOLASTIC INC.
New York Toronto London Auckland Sydney

A PARACHUTE PRESS BOOK

If you purchased this book without a cover, you should be aware that this book is stolen property. It was reported as "unsold and destroyed" to the publisher, and neither the author nor the publisher has received any payment for this "stripped book."

No part of this publication may be reproduced in whole or in part, or stored in a retrieval system, or transmitted in any form or by any means, electronic, mechanical, photocopying, recording, or otherwise, without written permission of the publisher. For information regarding permission, write to Scholastic Inc., 555 Broadway, New York, NY 10012.

ISBN 0-590-56888-4

Copyright © 1997 by Parachute Press, Inc.
All rights reserved. Published by Scholastic Inc.
APPLE PAPERBACKS and the APPLE PAPERBACKS logo are registered trademarks of Scholastic Inc.
GOOSEBUMPS is a registered trademark
of Parachute Press, Inc.

12 11 10 9 8 7 6 5 4 3 2 1   7 8 9/9 0 1 2/0

Printed in the U.S.A.   40

First Scholastic printing, January 1997

When the snows blow wild
And the day grows old,
Beware, the snowman, my child.
Beware, the snowman.
He brings the cold.

Why did that rhyme return to me?

It was a rhyme my mother used to whisper to me when I was a little girl. I could almost hear Mom's soft voice, a voice I haven't heard since I was five. . . .

Beware, the snowman.
He brings the cold.

Mom died when I was five, and I went to live with my aunt Greta. I'm twelve now, and my aunt never read that rhyme to me.

So what made it run through my mind as Aunt Greta and I climbed out of the van and gazed at our snow-covered new home?

"Jaclyn, you look troubled," Aunt Greta said,

placing a hand on the shoulder of my blue parka. "What are you thinking about, dear?"

I shivered. Not from Aunt Greta's touch, but from the chill of the steady wind that blew down from the mountain. I stared at the flat-roofed cabin that was to be our new home.

Beware, the snowman.

There is a second verse to that rhyme, I thought. Why can't I remember it?

I wondered if we still had the old poetry book that Mom used to read to me from.

"What a cozy little home," Aunt Greta said. She still had her hand on my shoulder.

I felt so sad, so terribly unhappy. But I forced a smile to my face. "Yes. Cozy," I murmured. Snow clung to the windowsills and filled the cracks between the shingles. A mound of snow rested on the low, flat roof.

Aunt Greta's normally pale cheeks were red from the cold. She isn't very old, but she has had white hair for as long as I can remember. She wears it long, always tied behind her head in a single braid that falls nearly all the way down her back.

She is tall and skinny. And kind of pretty, with a delicate round face and big, sad dark eyes.

I don't look at all like my aunt. I don't know *who* I look like. I don't remember my mom that well. And I never knew my father. Aunt Greta told me he disappeared soon after I was born.

2

I have wavy, dark brown hair and brown eyes. I am tall and athletic. I was the star basketball player on the girls' team at my school back in Chicago.

I like to talk a lot and dance and sing. Aunt Greta can go a whole day without barely saying a word. I love her, but she's so stern and silent. . . . Sometimes I wish she were easier to talk to.

I'm going to need someone to talk to, I thought sadly. We had left Chicago only yesterday. But I already missed my friends.

How am I going to make friends in this tiny village on the edge of the Arctic Circle? I wondered.

I helped my aunt pull bags from the van. My boots crunched over the hard snow.

I gazed up at the snow-covered mountain. Snow, snow everywhere. I couldn't tell where the mountain ended and the clouds began.

The little square houses along the road didn't look real to me. They looked as if they were made of gingerbread.

As if I had stepped into some kind of fairy tale.

Except it wasn't a fairy tale. It was my life.

My totally weird life.

I mean, why did we have to move from the United States to this tiny, frozen mountain village?

Aunt Greta never really explained. "Time for a change," she muttered. "Time to move on." It was so hard to get her to say more than a few words at a time.

3

I knew that she and Mom grew up in a village like this one. But why did we have to move here now? Why did I have to leave my school and all of my friends?

Sherpia.

What kind of a name is Sherpia? Can you *imagine* moving from Chicago to *Sherpia*?

Lucky, huh?

No way.

It isn't even a skiing town. The whole village is practically deserted! I wondered if there was anyone here my age.

Aunt Greta kicked snow away from the front door of our new house. Then she struggled to open the door. "The wood is warped," she grunted. She lowered her shoulder to the door — and pushed it open.

She's thin, but she's tough.

I started to carry the bags into the house. But something standing in the snowy yard across the road caught my eye. Curious, I turned and stared at it.

I gasped as it came into focus.

What *is* that?

A snowman?

A snowman with a *scar*?

As I squinted across the road at it, the snowman started to move.

2

I blinked.

No. The snowman wasn't moving.

Its red scarf was fluttering in the swirling breeze.

My boots crunched loudly as I stepped up to the snowman and examined it carefully.

What a *weird* snowman. It had slender tree limbs for arms. One arm poked out to the side. The other arm stood straight up, as if waving to me. Each tree limb had three twig fingers poking out from it.

The snowman had two dark, round stones for eyes. A crooked carrot nose. And a down-turned, sneering mouth of smaller pebbles.

Why did they make it so mean looking? I wondered.

I couldn't take my eyes off the scar. It was long and deep, cut down the right side of the snowman's face.

"Weird," I muttered out loud. My favorite

word. Aunt Greta is always saying I need a bigger vocabulary.

But how else would you describe a nasty-looking, sneering snowman with a scar on its face?

"Jaclyn — come help!" Aunt Greta's call made me turn away from the snowman. I hurried back across the road to my new house.

It took a long while to unpack the van. When we lugged the final carton into the cabin, Aunt Greta found a pot. Then she made us hot chocolate on the little, old-fashioned stove in the kitchen.

"Cozy," she repeated. She smiled. But her dark eyes studied my face. I think she was trying to see if I was unhappy.

"At least it's warm in here," she said, wrapping her bony fingers around the white hot-chocolate mug. Her cheeks were still red from the cold.

I nodded sullenly. I wanted to cheer up. But I just couldn't. I kept thinking about my friends back home. I wondered if they were going to a Bulls game tonight. My friends were all into basketball.

I won't be playing much basketball here, I thought unhappily. Even if they play basketball, there probably aren't enough kids in the village for a team!

"You'll be warm up there," Aunt Greta said, cutting into my thoughts. She pointed up to the low ceiling.

6

The house had only one bedroom. That was my aunt's room. My room was the low attic beneath the roof.

"I'm going to check it out," I said, pushing back my chair. It scraped on the hardwood floor.

The only way to reach my room was a metal ladder that stood against the wall. I climbed the ladder, then pushed away the flat board in the ceiling and pulled myself into the low attic.

It was *cozy*, all right. My aunt had picked the right word.

The ceiling was so low, I couldn't stand up. Pale, white light streamed in through the one small, round window at the far end of the room.

Crouching, I made my way to the window and peered out. Snow speckled the windowpane. But I could see the road and the two rows of little houses curving up the mountainside.

I didn't see anyone out there. Not a soul.

I'll bet they've all gone to Florida, I thought glumly.

It was midwinter break. The school here was closed. Aunt Greta and I had passed it on our way through the village. A small, gray stone building, not much bigger than a two-car garage.

How many kids will be in my class? I wondered. Three or four? Just me? And will they all speak English?

I swallowed hard. And scolded myself for being so down.

7

Cheer up, Jaclyn, I thought. Sherpia is a beautiful little village. You might meet some really neat kids here.

Ducking my head, I made my way back to the ladder. I'm going to cover the ceiling with posters, I decided. That will brighten this attic a lot.

And maybe help cheer me up, too.

"Can I help unpack?" I asked Aunt Greta as I climbed down the ladder.

She pushed her long, white braid off her shoulder. "No. I want to work in the kitchen first. Why don't you take a walk or something? Do a little exploring."

A few minutes later, I found myself outside, pulling the drawstrings of my parka hood tight. I adjusted my fur-lined gloves and waited for my eyes to adjust to the white glare of the snow.

Which way should I walk? I wondered.

I had already seen the school, the general store, a small church, and the post office down the road. So I decided to head *up* the road, toward the mountaintop.

The snow was hard and crusty. My boots hardly made a dent in it as I leaned into the wind and started to walk. Tire tracks cut twin ruts down the middle of the road. I decided to walk in one of them.

I passed a couple of houses about the same size as ours. They both appeared dark and empty. A tall, stone house had a Jeep parked in the driveway.

I saw a kid's sled in the front yard. An old-fashioned wooden sled. A yellow-eyed, black cat stared out at me from the living-room window.

I waved a gloved hand at it. It didn't move.

I still hadn't seen any other humans.

The wind whistled and grew colder as I climbed. The road grew steeper as it curved up. The houses were set farther apart.

The snow sparkled as clouds rolled away from the sun. It was suddenly so beautiful! I turned and gazed down at the houses I had passed, little gingerbread houses nestled in the snow.

It's so pretty, I thought. Maybe I *will* get to like it here.

"Ohh!" I cried out as I felt icy fingers wrap themselves around my neck.

3

I spun around and pulled free of the frozen grip.

And stared at a grinning boy in a brown sheepskin jacket and a red-and-green wool ski cap. "Did I scare you?" he asked. His grin grew wider.

Before I could answer, a girl about my age stepped out from behind a broad evergreen bush. She wore a purple down coat and purple gloves.

"Don't mind Eli," she said, tossing her hair off her face. "He's a total creep."

"Thanks for the compliment," Eli grinned.

I decided they must be brother and sister. They both had round faces, straight black hair, and bright, sky-blue eyes.

"You're new," Eli said, squinting at me.

"Eli thinks it's funny to scare any new kids," his sister told me, rolling her eyes. "My little brother is a riot, isn't he?"

"Being scared is about all there is to do in Sherpia," Eli said. His grin faded.

What a weird thing to say, I thought.

I introduced myself. "I'm Jaclyn DeForest," I told them. Their names were Rolonda and Eli Browning.

"We live there," Eli said, pointing to the white house. "Where do you live?"

I pointed down the road. "Farther down," I replied. I started to ask them something — but stopped when I saw the snowman they were building.

It had one arm out and one arm up. It had a red scarf wrapped under its head. And it had a deep scar cut down the right side of its face.

"That s-snowman —" I stammered. "It looks just like one I saw across the street from me."

Rolonda's smile faded. Eli lowered his eyes to the snow. "Really?" he muttered.

"Why did you make it like that?" I demanded. "It's so strange looking. Why did you put that scar on its face?"

They glanced at each other tensely.

They didn't reply.

Finally, Rolonda shrugged. "I really don't know," she murmured. She blushed.

Was she lying? Why didn't she want to answer me?

"Where are you walking?" Eli asked, tightening the snowman's red scarf.

"Just walking," I told him. "Do you guys want

to come with me? I thought I'd walk up to the top of the mountain."

"*No!*" Eli gasped. His blue eyes widened in fear.

"You *can't!*" Rolonda cried. "You *can't!*"

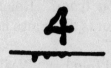

4

"Excuse me?"

I gaped at them in shock. What was their *problem*?

"Why can't I go up to the top?" I demanded.

The fear faded quickly from their faces. Rolonda tossed back her black hair. Eli pretended to be busy with the red snowman scarf.

"You can't go because it's closed for repairs," Eli finally replied.

"Ha ha. Remind me to laugh later," Rolonda sneered.

"So what's the real reason?" I demanded.

"Uh . . . well . . . we just never go up there," Rolonda stammered, glancing at her brother. She waited for Eli to add something. But he didn't.

"It's kind of like a tradition," Rolonda continued, avoiding my eyes. "I mean . . . well . . . we just don't go up there."

"It's too cold," Eli added. "That's why. It's just

too cold up there for humans to survive. You would turn to ice in thirty seconds."

I knew he was lying. I knew that wasn't the real reason. But I decided to drop the subject. They suddenly seemed so tense and worried.

"Where are you from?" Rolonda asked. She dug her gloved hands deep into her coat pockets. "The next village?"

"No. Chicago," I told her. "We lived in an apartment right on the lake."

"And you moved *here*?" Eli cried. "From Chicago to Sherpia? *Why*?"

"Good question," I muttered, rolling my eyes. "I live with my aunt, see. And Aunt Greta decided to move here. So . . ." I couldn't keep the sadness from my voice.

We talked for a few more minutes. I learned that they had lived in Sherpia their entire lives. "It isn't so bad. You get used to not seeing many people," Rolonda told me.

"And it's nice if you like snow," Eli added. "Lots and lots of snow!"

We all laughed.

I said, "See you guys later," and started walking up the road.

"You're not going to the top — are you?" Eli called. He sounded really frightened again.

"No," I called back. I pulled my hood tight. "It's getting kind of windy. I'll just go a little farther."

The road curved higher. I crunched my way

past a wide, woodsy lot filled with pine trees nearly as thin as pencils. The trees tilted at all angles. Not one of them stood straight up.

I saw animal tracks in the snow. Raccoon or squirrel? No. Too big. Deer tracks? I couldn't tell.

I raised my eyes — and cried out in surprise.

Another sneering snowman stared back at me with its twisted carrot nose and coal-black eyes.

Its red scarf fluttered in the strong wind.

I stared at the long scar cut deep in its face.

Its twig arms waved in the wind, as if greeting me.

"Why do they build these creepy snowmen?" I asked out loud.

I turned — and saw another one in the front yard across the street. Same tree-branch arms. Same red scarf. Same scar.

It must be some kind of village decoration, I decided.

But why didn't Rolonda and Eli want to tell me about it?

Heavy gray clouds rolled over the sun. The snowman's shadow appeared to stretch until it swept over me.

I felt a sudden chill. I stepped back.

The sky quickly turned evening dark. I gazed up to the top of the mountain. Clumps of pine trees hid the top from view.

Should I head back or keep going?

I remembered the fear on Eli's face when I said

I was climbing to the top. And I remembered Rolonda's cry: "You *can't*!"

It only made me more curious.

What were they afraid of? What was up there?

I decided to keep going.

A van in the next driveway was buried under a thick sheet of snow. It looked as if it hadn't been driven all winter.

I followed the road as it curved away from the houses. The snow became deeper and softer. My boots sank in as I walked.

I imagined that I was walking on another planet, a planet never explored before.

The road climbed steeper. Large white rocks jutted up from the snow. Clumps of slender pine trees tilted in every direction.

There were no houses up this high. I could see only trees and snow-covered shrubs and jutting rocks.

The road curved again. The wind whistled. I rubbed my cheeks and nose to warm them. Then I leaned into the wind and kept walking.

I stopped when a small log cabin came into view. I shielded my eyes with a gloved hand and stared at it.

A cabin way up here?

Why would anyone want to live this high up, away from everyone?

The cabin stood in a square, cleared-out area,

surrounded by scraggly, tilting pine trees. I didn't see any car or sled. I didn't see any boot-prints in the snow.

I crept closer to the cabin.

The windows were steamed over. I couldn't tell if there were lights on inside or not.

I stepped closer, my heart pounding. I leaned my arms on a windowsill and pressed my nose against the glass. But I couldn't see in.

"Anyone home?" I called.

Silence. The wind whistled around the corner of the cabin.

I knocked on the door. "Hello?"

No reply.

"Weird," I muttered.

I tried the door. I just pushed it lightly.

Maybe I shouldn't have. But I did.

The door slid open.

I felt a rush of warm air from inside.

"Anyone home?" I called in.

I peeked beyond the door. Dark in there.

"Hello?"

I stepped inside. Just to take a look.

The snow had been so bright outside. My eyes adjusted slowly to the dim light.

And before I could focus, I saw a white blur.

A *growling* white blur. It leaped on me.

Hot breath. Hot breath on my face.

And a snarling, white creature tackled me to the floor.

5

"Down! Down, Wolfbane!"

The snarling stopped instantly.

The creature backed off.

"Down, Wolfbane!" a man's voice ordered sternly.

Gasping for breath, I wiped hot saliva off my face. And realized I was staring up at a white-furred wolf.

The wolf was breathing hard, too, jaws open, tongue snaking down nearly to the cabin floor. Its head was lowered as if preparing to attack again. Its round, dark brown eyes locked on me suspiciously.

"Down, Wolfbane. It's okay, boy."

I rolled away from the panting creature and climbed to my knees. Two hands reached down to grab my hands and tug me to my feet.

"Are you okay?" The man studied me with round, silver-gray eyes. He was tall and thin, dressed all in denim. He had long, gray hair tied back in a short ponytail. And a thick, pure-white beard.

His eyes glowed like steel marbles. I could almost *feel* them burning into me.

"Is that . . . really a wolf?" I demanded.

He nodded, his expression stern, his eerie eyes not moving, not blinking. "He won't hurt you. Wolfbane is well trained."

"But he —" My mouth suddenly felt so dry it was hard to talk.

"You startled us," the man said, still not blinking, not looking away. "We were in the back room." He motioned toward a doorway in the back wall.

"Sorry," I murmured. "I didn't know anyone was in here. I thought —"

"Who *are* you?" the man demanded angrily. He narrowed his silvery eyes at me. Behind the bushy white beard, his slender face reddened.

"I didn't mean to —"

"Who *are* you?" he repeated.

"I was taking a walk," I struggled to explain. If only my heart weren't pounding so hard. If only my mouth weren't so dry.

The white wolf uttered a low growl. It stood tensely, head lowered, eyes locked on me, as if waiting for a command to attack.

"Why did you break into my house?" the man demanded, taking a step toward me.

He's dangerous, I realized.

There's something very strange about him. Something very angry.

"I didn't break in," I started. "I just —"

"You broke into my house," he insisted. "Don't you realize how dangerous that is? Wolfbane is trained to attack strangers."

"S-sorry — !" I choked out.

He took another step toward me. He still hadn't blinked those weird, round eyes.

My chest tightened in fright.

What did he plan to do?

I didn't want to find out.

I took a deep breath. Then I spun around — and ran out the door.

Could I get away?

Behind me, the door slammed hard against the cabin wall.

I glanced back — and saw him burst out of the cabin after me. "Where are you going?" he cried. "Hey — stop! Where are you going?"

I pointed. "Up to the top!" I cried.

"No, you're not!" he shouted back furiously. "You will not go up there!"

He's crazy! I realized.

He has no right to shout at me like that!

I can go anywhere I want to!

He's crazy.

It had started to snow, large wet flakes, blowing hard in swirls of wind.

I brushed a snowflake from my forehead and ran to the road.

To my horror, the bearded man followed me, half-walking, half-running over the deep snow.

"Beware, the snowman!" he called.

"Huh?" I turned back to face him. "What did you say?" I cried breathlessly.

The old rhyme flew through my mind for the second time that day . . .

When the snows blow wild
And the day grows old,
Beware, the snowman, my child.
Beware, the snowman.
He brings the cold.

I don't *believe* this! I thought. I haven't thought about that rhyme since I was five. And now it has run through my mind *twice* in one day!

We stood staring at each other from opposite sides of the road. I saw the man shiver. He wore only his denim workshirt, no coat. Big snowflakes clung to his gray hair and his shoulders.

"What did you say?" I asked.

"The snowman lives in the ice cave," he called, cupping his hands around his mouth to be heard over the wind.

"Huh? A snowman?"

He's really nuts! I decided. Why am I standing here listening to him?

The man lives in a cabin on a mountaintop all by himself except for a white wolf! And now he's yelling insane things about a snowman!

"Beware, the snowman!" he repeated. "You cannot go up to the top! You cannot!"

"Why not?" I demanded. My voice came out higher and more shrill than I had intended.

"You do not want to meet the snowman!" the man cried. The big snowflakes covered his beard. His silvery eyes glowed eerily.

"If you meet the snowman," he called, *"you will never return!"*

Totally nuts, I realized.

That's why he lives all alone up here.

I spun away. I knew I had stayed too long.

Slipping and sliding, I ran through the deep snow.

Ran as fast as I could. Cold snowflakes slapping my hot face. Heart pounding.

Down the road. Down the curving mountain road.

Panting . . . panting.

Was that *me* breathing so hard?

Were those *my* thudding footsteps?

No.

Glancing back, I saw the white wolf chasing me. Gaining fast.

Teeth bared. Head lowered to attack.

"Noooo!" I wailed. The big snowflakes stung my eyes as I ran. The white ground tilted. I stumbled but kept running.

I suddenly felt as if I were trapped in one of those glass balls that snows inside when you shake them.

I tumbled downhill. The snowflakes flew at me

in all directions. The whole mountainside seemed to quiver and shake.

The road! Where was the road?

I lost it in the falling snow. My boots sank into deep drifts.

But I kept running. Down . . . down.

The steady thud of the wolf's heavy paws in my ears.

I glanced back and saw it gaining on me, moving rhythmically, easily over the snowdrifts. Its teeth were bared. Puffs of steam rose from its open mouth.

Running hard, I didn't see the smooth rocks jutting up along the side of the road.

My boot caught on one.

"Ohhhh!" I let out a cry as pain shot up my leg. I lost my balance. Stumbled forward.

Landed hard on my stomach in the deep snow.

I gasped for breath. The fall knocked the wind out of me.

Scrambling to my knees, I watched helplessly as the white wolf closed in on me.

7

To my surprise, the wolf stopped a few feet away.

It lowered its head and stared, breathing hard. Beneath the thick, white fur, its chest heaved up and down. Snowflakes melted on its tongue.

Staring at it in fear, I pushed myself to my feet. I brushed my hair back, and brushed snow off the front of my parka.

Was the wolf just catching its breath? Would it attack the moment I tried to run?

"Go home, boy," I whispered. "Go home."

My voice barely carried over the wind and snow. The white wolf stared up at me, still panting.

I started to back up. I was afraid to take my eyes off it.

I took one step back. Then another.

The wolf watched me but didn't move.

My boots crunched onto the road. Yes! I had found the road! I kept backing up.

The wolf stood taller. Lowered its tail. Tensed its back.

Its brown eyes followed me. Such human eyes.

What was it thinking? Why did it chase after me?

Was it just making sure that I went down the mountain? Did the strange man send it to keep me from heading to the mountaintop?

I took another step back. Then another.

The wolf didn't move.

The snow-covered road curved away. I kept backing up until I was out of the creature's sight.

"Whew!" I uttered a loud sigh of relief. Turned. And continued walking fast toward the village and my new house.

Every few seconds, I glanced back. But the wolf didn't follow me.

The snow came down hard. I pulled my parka hood over my hair. I held it with both hands and started to trot along the road.

I wondered if Aunt Greta would be worried about me. I had been gone a lot longer than I had planned.

Low snow clouds hid the sun. The sky became nearly as black as night.

I started to pass houses on both sides of the road. I could see lights on in some of them. One house had a blazing fire going in a fireplace. Black smoke curled up from the chimney.

I passed one of the strange, scar-faced snowmen. His tree-limb arms trembled in the wind. He appeared to be waving at me as I passed.

I broke into a run.

Another snowman greeted me as I rounded the next curve.

I hate this village! I thought.

It's too weird. Too weird!

I'm never going to be happy here. Never!

Why did Aunt Greta bring us here?

A thudding sound behind me forced away my unhappy thoughts.

I'm being followed! I realized.

The wolf?

No. These heavy footsteps were different.

Human footsteps.

The crazy, bearded man — he followed me!

"Ohhh!" A frightened moan escaped my lips.

Taking a deep breath, I spun around to face him.

"Jaclyn — hi!"

I gasped — and stared through the falling snow at Rolonda. She jogged across the road to me. Snowflakes dotted her black hair.

"You ran right past our house," she said breathlessly, pointing to her yard. "Didn't you see us?"

I glanced over her shoulder and saw her brother, Eli, waving to me from their driveway.

"No. I . . . uh . . . the snow was falling so hard, and —" I stammered.

"Are you okay?" Rolonda demanded.

"Well . . ." I hesitated. "A white wolf chased me," I blurted out. "A crazy man. He has a cabin near the top. His wolf chased me and he —"

"You ran into Conrad?" Rolonda cried.

"Huh? Conrad?" The wind blew my hood off my head. I squinted hard at Rolonda. "Is that his name?"

She nodded. "He has a cabin that he built hir.

self. And he keeps a white wolf named Wolfbane. I meant to warn you before, Jaclyn —"

"Warn me?" I interrupted.

"Yeah. To stay away from him. He and that animal he keeps — they're both really strange."

"Tell me about it!" I groaned. I rolled my eyes. "Is that why you and Eli never go up to the mountaintop?"

Rolonda lowered her eyes. "Well . . . it's *one* of the reasons."

I waited for her to go on. But she didn't. She continued to stare down at the snow. She kicked a clump of wet snow off one boot with the other. Behind her, Eli stood watching us, his hands jammed into his coat pockets.

"Well, why does Conrad live up there so far away from everyone?" I demanded.

Rolonda hesitated. She glanced back tensely at her brother. "No one knows for sure," she answered finally. "He — maybe he works for the snowman. I mean . . ." Her voice trailed off.

"Excuse me?" I cried. I was sure I hadn't heard her correctly. "What did you say, Rolonda? He works for the *snowman*? What do you mean? What does that *mean*?"

She didn't answer. Again, she glanced back nervously at Eli.

"Come on, Rolonda. What do you mean?" I insisted. "What do you mean, he works for the snowman?"

She backed away, brushing snowflakes from her hair. "I've got to go inside," she said. "It's almost dinnertime."

I followed after her. "But first you have to explain," I demanded.

"I *can't*," she whispered. "Because of Eli. He's too frightened."

"But, Rolonda —" I started. I saw Eli watching us intently from the driveway.

"Go home," Rolonda snapped. "Just go home, Jaclyn."

"Not until you tell me what you meant." I can be stubborn when I want to be.

"Okay, okay," she whispered, glancing over her shoulder at Eli. "Meet me tomorrow night, okay? Meet me tomorrow night at the church — and I'll tell you everything."

9

"Hi — I'm back!"

I burst into the house. Aunt Greta was bending over a carton in the small kitchen, pulling out coffee mugs and placing them in a cabinet. She spun around as I walked in.

"Is it snowing?" she asked.

I nodded my head furiously, tossing snowflakes from my hair. "The biggest flakes I ever saw," I replied breathlessly.

Aunt Greta frowned. "I've been so busy in here, I didn't even look out the window."

I pulled off my coat and carried it to the front closet. But there were no hangers in the closet yet. So I tossed the wet coat on top of a stack of cartons.

Then I walked back into the kitchen, rubbing the sleeves of my sweater. "Aunt Greta, do you know anything about a snowman?" I asked.

I heard her gasp.

But when she turned to me, her face was a blank. "Snowman?"

"Do you know anything about a snowman on top of the mountain?" I asked.

Aunt Greta bit her bottom lip. "No. No, I don't, Jaclyn." Her voice trembled. Why did she look so tense?

She bent down to pull more mugs from the carton. I crossed the room to help her unpack them.

"Someone told me I shouldn't go to the top of the mountain because of a snowman," I told her. "A snowman who *lives* up there."

Aunt Greta didn't say anything. She handed me two mugs. I lifted them onto the cabinet shelf.

"This man told me that if I met the snowman up there, I would never return," I continued.

My aunt let out a short, dry laugh. "Village superstition," she muttered.

I squinted at her. "Really?"

"Of course," she replied. "These tiny villages all have their scary stories. Someone was just having fun, giving you a little scare."

"Fun?" I frowned. "I don't think so."

That weird, white-bearded guy, Conrad, had screamed at me that I couldn't go up to the mountaintop. He wasn't joking. I knew he wasn't joking.

He was serious. He was *threatening* me. He wasn't having a little fun. No way.

"Aunt Greta, do you remember a rhyme about a snowman?" I asked.

She straightened up and stretched, pushing her hands against her back. "Rhyme?"

"I remembered a rhyme today. From when I was little. It just popped into my head."

Aunt Greta chewed her lip again fretfully. "I don't think I remember any rhyme," she said. She glanced away, avoiding my eyes.

"I only remember the first verse," I told her. And then I recited it:

"When the snows blow wild
And the day grows old,
Beware, the snowman, my child.
Beware, the snowman.
He brings the cold."

When I finished, I looked up to find the strangest expression on Aunt Greta's face. Her eyes had gone all watery. And her chin trembled. Her cheeks were even paler than usual.

"Aunt Greta — are you okay?" I asked. "What's wrong?"

"Nothing," she replied sharply, turning her face away from me. "Nothing at all, Jaclyn. But I don't remember that rhyme. I don't think I've ever heard it before."

She fiddled nervously with her long, white braid.

"Are you sure?" I asked timidly.

"Of *course* I'm sure," she snapped. "Now, come on. Help me finish up in here so I can begin dinner."

What is wrong? I wondered. Why is she suddenly angry at me?

And why do I have the feeling that she isn't telling the truth?

Aunt Greta has never lied to me before.

Why is she acting so strange now?

10

I couldn't sleep that night.

My new bed felt hard. I kept imagining that the low ceiling was sinking, dropping down on me.

The snow clouds had drifted away, and a half moon appeared, low in the sky. The moonlight washed in through my round window, casting long, shifting shadows over my room.

I shuddered under my quilt. It was all so new and strange. I wondered if I'd ever be able to sleep up here.

I shut my eyes and tried to think nice, soothing thoughts. I pictured my friends back in Chicago. I called up their faces one by one. I wondered what they were all doing today while I was having my frightening adventure on the mountain.

I wondered if they missed me.

I had just about fallen asleep when the howls began.

Wolf howls?

I climbed out of bed and made my way to the window. Down below, the moonlight made the snow sparkle, almost as bright as during the day.

Bushes trembled in a soft breeze. The wind carried another frightening howl. I raised my eyes to the mountain. But I could see only houses, dark and silent, and the silvery road that curved its way to the top.

My whole body tingled. I knew I couldn't fall asleep. It was chilly up here in my little attic room, and the air felt heavy and damp.

I decided to take a walk. Maybe it will help me relax, I told myself.

I pulled on a pair of jeans and a sweatshirt. Then I crept downstairs — careful not to wake Aunt Greta — and found my parka and boots.

Stepping out into the night, I silently closed the front door behind me. My eyes swept over the glittering snow of the small front yard.

I made my way to the road, my breath streaming up in wisps of fog. "Wow!" I murmured. "Wow!"

The cold, fresh air felt so good on my face.

The wind had stopped. The whole world seemed still and silent.

No cars, I realized. No horns honking. No buses roaring past. No people laughing and shouting on the street.

I'm all alone out here, I told myself. The whole world is *mine*.

A long, frightening howl brought me out of my crazy thoughts.

I shivered and raised my eyes to the mountain-top. Was the white wolf howling up there? Did it howl like that *every* night?

Why did the howls sound so human?

I took a deep breath of cold air and held it. Then I began walking slowly along the road. My boots crunched on the hard, crusty snow. I passed a few houses and kept walking.

I stopped as a shadow slid over my path.

11

I gasped. At first, I thought someone was following me.

But then I realized I was staring at a long shadow of a snowman. The shadow tilted over the road. The tree branch arms, one raised, one out to the side, appeared long and menacing.

I stepped over the shadow and crossed the street. But another shadow fell over me.

Another snowman. An identical snowman.

The shadows of the strange snowmen fell over each other. I suddenly felt as if I were walking in a black-and-white world of shadowy heads, fluttering scarves, and sticklike arms — all saluting, all waving.

Why were there so many of them?

Why did the people in this village build them all alike?

Another howl made me raise my eyes from the crisscrossing shadows over the snow. This howl sounded closer. And it definitely sounded human!

A chill ran down my back.

I turned. Time to head home, I decided.

My heart was pounding now. The howl — so near — had really frightened me.

I started to walk fast, swinging my arms as I walked, leaning into the gusting wind.

But I stopped when I saw the scarfaced snowman in the driveway up ahead.

And I gasped when it nodded its head at me.

"Noooo!" A low cry escaped my lips.

It nodded. The snowman nodded!

Then the head rolled to the ground. And cracked apart with a soft *thud*.

And I realized the wind had made its head nod. The wind had blown the scarred head off the body.

What am I *doing* out here? I asked myself. It's late and it's cold.

And it's weird.

And some kind of creature nearby is howling its head off.

I gazed across the yard at the headless snowman. The head was a shattered clump of white at the snowman's base. But the scarf had remained on top of the round body. It flapped in a gust of cold wind.

I felt another shiver. I turned and ran toward home.

Ran through the blue-black shadows of snow-men. My boots crunched over the shadows of their waving arms, their scarred heads.

A snowman in each yard. Snowmen lining the street like night watchmen.

This walk was a crazy idea, I thought, feeling panic tighten my chest. I want to be home now. I want to be back in the safety of my new home.

A snowman waved its three-fingered limb at me and sneered its coal-dark sneer as I ran past. And as I scrambled for home, the rhyme forced its way back into my mind. . . .

When the snows blow wild
And the day grows old,
Beware, the snowman, my child.
Beware, the snowman.
He brings the cold.

My house came into view down the road. I sucked in a deep breath and ran harder.

The old rhyme had been haunting me ever since I arrived in the village. The old rhyme had followed me from my childhood, followed me to my strange, new home.

Why did I suddenly remember it today?

What was it trying to tell me? Why had the cold words returned after being forgotten for so many years?

I had to find the rest of it. I had to find the second verse of the poem.

An eerie howl, rising like an ambulance siren, sounded so close behind me I spun around.

I searched the road and the frozen yards. No one there. No wolf. No human.

Another howl sounded even closer.

Was someone following me?

I held my hands over my ears to keep out the frightening sounds — and I *flew* over the snow, flew the rest of the way home.

I reached the narrow front door as another long howl sent a chill down my body.

Closer. It's so close, I realized.

Someone *is* following me!

I grabbed the doorknob. Twisted it. Pushed.

No!

The door didn't budge.

I twisted again. This way. The other way.

Pushed the door. Pulled it.

Locked.

I had locked myself out!

12

Another frightening howl.

So close. From the side of my house!

My whole body trembled. Panic tightened my throat. I stumbled back from the front door.

And saw that the front window — the only window on this side of the house — was open a crack. Snow streaked the windowpanes and clumped on the narrow sill.

I stared at the tiny opening at the window bottom.

Then I sucked in a deep breath — and hurtled to the window.

I grabbed the snowy wooden frame. Uttering a loud groan, I pushed. Pushed up with all my strength.

To my surprise, the window slid up easily.

I pushed it all the way up. Then I grabbed the sill with both hands. I hoisted myself up, up — as another howl rang through the night air.

So close.

So close and frightening.

I tumbled headfirst into the house. Landed hard on my hands and knees on the wooden floor.

With a gasp, I scrambled to my feet. Grabbed the window and pulled it shut.

Then I stood, leaning against the wall, listening. Waiting to catch my breath.

Had I awakened Aunt Greta?

No. The house stood dark and silent. The only sound I could hear was my rapid, shallow breathing.

Another howl, distant this time.

Had I only imagined that I was being followed? Were the terrifying howls rolling down from the mountaintop, carried by the wind?

Still breathing hard, I stepped away from the front wall. Making my way slowly through the darkness, I headed to the little back room where we had piled all of the packing cartons.

My books were still stuffed in one of the cartons.

I was sure that I had packed the old poetry book Mom used to read to me.

White moonlight flooded in from the window against the back wall. I found the book carton on top of a stack and pulled it down to the floor.

My hands trembled as I struggled to pull off the heavy packing tape and open the box.

I have to find that poem, I told myself. I have to read the second verse of that rhyme.

I tugged open the carton and began pulling out books. I had packed a bunch of paperbacks on the top. Underneath them, I found some textbooks and anthologies I had used at school.

As I pulled them out and stacked them carefully on the floor, I heard a cough.

And then a footstep.

Someone else is in here! I realized.

"Aunt Greta? Is that you?" I cried.

But the voice that replied wasn't Aunt Greta's.

"What are you doing?" a strange voice demanded in a raspy whisper.

13

The ceiling light flashed on.

I blinked.

Swallowed hard.

And stared up at Aunt Greta.

"You frightened me, Jaclyn!" she croaked.

I jumped to my feet. "You frightened me, too!" I replied, waiting for my heart to stop pounding. "What happened to your voice?"

Aunt Greta rubbed her pale throat. "I've lost it," she rasped. "Horrible sore throat. It must be the cold. I'm not used to the cold of this village yet."

Her straight, white hair hung loose behind her. She tugged it off the collar of her flannel night-shirt, brushing out tangles with one hand. "What are you doing, Jaclyn? Why are you down here in the middle of the night?" she croaked.

"That old poem," I replied. "I want to find it. I can't remember the second verse. I —"

"We'll unpack the books tomorrow," she cut in.

She yawned. "I'm so tired. And my throat hurts so badly. Let's try to get some sleep."

She suddenly appeared so tiny and frail.

"I'm sorry," I said, following her from the room. "I didn't mean to wake you up. I couldn't sleep, so . . ."

Her eyes fell on my parka, which I had tossed onto a living room chair. "You went out?" she cried, spinning to face me. I could see alarm on her face.

"Well . . . yes," I confessed. "I thought maybe a short walk . . ."

"You shouldn't go out in the middle of the night," she scolded. She rubbed her sore throat. Her eyes narrowed at me.

"Sorry," I muttered. "What's the big deal, anyway? What's so terrible about going out at night?"

She hesitated, chewing her lower lip the way she always does when she's thinking hard. "It's just dangerous. That's all," she whispered finally. "What if you fell in the snow or something? What if you broke your leg? There is no one outside to help you."

"I'd roll home!" I joked. I laughed but she didn't join in.

I had the strong feeling she had something else on her mind. She wasn't worried about me falling down. She was worried about something else.

But she didn't want to say it.

46

Did it have anything to do with the animal howls?

Did it have something to do with the snowman on the mountain that Conrad had warned me about? The snowman that Aunt Greta said was just a village superstition?

I yawned. I finally felt sleepy. Too sleepy to think any more about these questions.

I put my arm around Aunt Greta's slender shoulders and walked her across the hall to her room. "Sorry I woke you," I whispered. Then I said good night and climbed the ladder to my attic bedroom.

Yawning, I pulled off my jeans and sweatshirt and tossed them on the floor. Then I jumped into bed and pulled the quilt up to my chin.

Pale moonlight washed in from the round window at the other end of the room. I shut my eyes. No howls outside. No sounds at all.

I snuggled my head into my soft pillow. My new bed still felt hard. But I was too tired to care.

I had just about drifted off to sleep when the whispered words floated into the room. . . .

"Beware, the snowman, Jaclyn. . . . Beware, the snowman. . . ."

14

I sat straight up with a gasp. "Huh? Who's there?" I choked out.

I stared across the room at the window. The unfamiliar shapes of my furniture appeared silvery, ghostlike in the white moonlight.

"*Beware, the snowman....*" the whispered words were repeated. "*Jaclyn, beware, the snowman.*"

"Who are you?" I cried. "How do you know my name?"

Sitting up in the strange bed, I grabbed the end of the quilt, gripping it tightly in both hands, squeezing it.

And I listened.

Silence now.

"Who *are* you?" My cry so tiny and shrill.

Silence.

"Who *are* you?"

Silence . . .

I don't know how long I sat there, waiting for a

reply. But after a while, I somehow drifted off to sleep.

The next morning I told Aunt Greta about the whispered warning.

She sipped her coffee before replying. Then she reached across the table and squeezed my hand. "I had bad dreams, too, last night," she said, still whispering because of her sore throat.

"Dream?" I replied. "Do you think it was a dream?"

Aunt Greta nodded and took another long sip of coffee. "Of course," she croaked.

I spent the day helping my aunt unpack the cartons and arrange our new house. I searched every carton for the poetry book, but I couldn't find it. I didn't realize how much stuff we had brought from our apartment in Chicago. Such a small house. It was a real struggle to find a place for everything.

As we worked, I found myself thinking about Rolonda. She had promised to meet me at the little village church after dinner. She said she would tell me the truth about the snowman tonight.

The truth . . .

I pictured her brother Eli's frightened expression as he stood in the snowy driveway, watching Rolonda and me. And I remembered how frightened they became when I told them I was walking to the mountaintop.

49

So much fear here in this village. Was it all because of silly superstitions?

After I washed and dried the dinner dishes, I pulled on my parka and my boots and prepared to meet Rolonda. I told Aunt Greta the truth. I told her I was meeting a village girl my age I'd met during my walk.

"It's snowing really hard," Aunt Greta said in her raspy whisper. "Don't stay out late, Jaclyn."

I promised I'd be home before nine. Then I pulled up my hood, tugged on my gloves, and stepped outside.

Does it snow here *every day*? I asked myself, shaking my head.

I've always liked snow. But *enough* already!

The snow came down hard, in sheets driven by a strong wind. I lowered my head and trudged down the road toward the church. Snowflakes blew into my face and stung my eyes. I could barely see.

What a blizzard!

I wondered if Rolonda would show up.

The little stone church stood across from the post office. It wasn't far down the road from my house. But walking into the blowing snow, it seemed miles away.

Keeping my head down, I stepped into a deep drift. Cold snow dropped into my boot, soaking my sock. "Ohhh." I let out a shuddering groan. "I'm going to *freeze*!" I cried out loud.

There was no one around to hear me. The road stood empty. Nothing moved. I passed a brightly-lit house, but I couldn't see anyone inside.

The snow blew against my face, my coat, as if trying to push me back. As if trying to make me turn around.

"This is crazy," I murmured. "Crazy. No *way* Rolonda will meet me tonight."

Squinting into the gray evening light, I saw the steeple of the church, white against the falling snow. "I hope it's open," I said out loud.

Ducking my head, I ran across the road — and thudded into something hard. And very cold.

Evil black eyes glared into mine.

And I started to scream.

15

A second later, hands jerked me away.

And a voice cried, "Jaclyn — what's wrong?"

My scream caught in my throat. I stumbled back, my boots slipping in the slick, wet snow.

I turned to see Rolonda, tugging on my coat sleeve. "I saw you run right into that snowman," she said. "But why did you scream?"

"I — I —" I sputtered. I squinted through the falling snow at the snowman, at his dark eyes, at the scar down his round face. "I — I just freaked," I stammered.

I scolded myself for acting so stupid. Now Rolonda must think I'm a real jerk, I thought unhappily.

What is wrong with me, anyway? Screaming because I bumped into a snowman!

"Why did someone build a snowman like that in front of the church?" I asked.

Rolonda didn't reply. Her dark eyes peered into mine. "Are you okay?" she asked.

I nodded. "Yeah. Fine. Let's get out of this snow."

I took one last glance at the sneering snowman. Then I followed Rolonda to a wooden door on the side of the small church. We stepped inside and stamped the snow off our boots on a straw mat.

"Does it *ever* stop snowing here?" I grumbled, pulling back my hood and unzipping my parka.

"Sure. It stopped once for ten minutes. We all took a summer vacation!" Rolonda joked. She shook out her long, black hair.

I glanced around. We were in some kind of waiting room. A long wooden bench stood against the back wall. Two lights shaped like old-fashioned gas lamps hung on the wall beside the bench, giving off a soft glow.

We dropped our coats beside the bench and sat down. I rubbed my hands, trying to warm them. My cheeks burned.

"It's nice and warm in here," Rolonda said, keeping her voice low. "The pastor keeps the heat up really high. He doesn't like to be cold."

"Who does?" I murmured, rubbing my ears, trying to return some feeling to them.

"It's a nice, quiet place to talk," Rolonda continued. "Especially to talk about things that are . . . kind of scary."

"Scary?" I replied.

She glanced around the small, white-walled

room. She suddenly seemed tense. Uncomfortable.

"Did your aunt tell you anything about the village?" Rolonda whispered. "Anything about the history of the village?"

I had to lean closer to hear her. She was whispering so softly.

Why is she so nervous? I wondered. We're the only ones in the entire church.

"No," I replied. "Not a thing. I really don't think Aunt Greta knows much about this village at all."

"Then why did you move here?" Rolonda demanded.

I shrugged. "Beats me. Aunt Greta never explained. She said it was time for us to leave Chicago."

Rolonda leaned forward tensely and brought her face close to mine. "I'll tell you the story," she whispered. "The history of this village is very strange. People don't talk about it much."

"Why not?" I interrupted.

"Because it's so frightening," Rolonda replied. "My brother, Eli, is terrified all the time. That's why I met you here at the church. He doesn't like for me to talk about any of this. He doesn't like for me to talk about the snowman."

"Snowman?" I demanded. I stared at her eagerly. "What *about* the snowman?"

16

Rolonda shifted her weight. The wooden bench creaked beneath us. She took a deep breath and began her story.

"Years ago, two sorcerers lived in this village. A man and a woman. Everyone knew they were sorcerers. But everyone left them alone."

"Were they *evil* sorcerers?" I interrupted.

Rolonda shook her head. "No. I don't think they were evil. At least, I don't think they meant to be."

She glanced around the room again. I settled back against the bench and waited impatiently for her to continue.

"One day, the two sorcerers were fooling around, having fun. They cast a spell on a snowman. And the snowman came to life."

I gasped. "Really?"

Rolonda narrowed her eyes at me. "Please, don't interrupt, Jaclyn. Please let me tell the whole story first."

I apologized.

Leaning close to me, she continued her story in a whisper.

"The sorcerers used their magic to bring the snowman to life. But then they lost control of it.

"The snowman was powerful. And it was evil. The sorcerers had given it life. But they didn't really know what they were doing. And they didn't know that the snowman would try to destroy the village and everyone in it.

"The sorcerers tried to use magic to put the snowman back to sleep. But their magic wasn't powerful enough.

"The villagers all gathered together. Somehow they managed to force the snowman up to the top of the mountain.

"There is a big cave at the very top of the mountain. The cave is cut in ice. Everyone calls it the ice cave.

"The villagers chased the evil snowman into the ice cave. Then most people moved away from the village. Few people wanted to stay, knowing that the evil creature was alive at the top of the mountain.

"So most people left," Rolonda continued, whispering so softly I could barely hear her. "The two sorcerers probably left, too. No one really knows what happened to them.

"And that's when Conrad comes into the story," Rolonda said.

I stared at her. "Conrad? The weird guy with the white beard?"

Rolonda nodded. "After the evil snowman was chased into the ice cave, Conrad moved up there. He built a cabin just beneath the ice cave. No one could figure out why.

"Is Conrad trying to protect the town?" Rolonda continued. "Does he work for the snowman? Does he help the snowman? Or does he think that living so close to the evil snowman will keep him safe?

"No one knows. Conrad very seldom comes down from the mountaintop. And when he does come into the village, he doesn't talk to anyone.

"No one knows for sure who he is or why he stays up there," Rolonda continued. "No one has anything to do with Conrad. We don't know if he's crazy or evil."

She sighed. Once again, her eyes darted around the room. She seemed so nervous, as if she didn't want anyone else to know that she was telling me the history of the village.

"Some nights," she continued, "we can hear the snowman up there on top of the mountain. Some nights we can hear him roaring and bellowing with rage. Some nights, we can hear him howling, howling like a wolf.

"We've all built snowmen. Snowmen that look like him. Everyone in the village builds them."

I jumped to my feet. "So *that's* why I see those weird snowmen everywhere!" I cried.

Rolonda raised a finger to her lips. She motioned for me to sit back down.

I dropped back onto the bench. "Why do you build the snowmen?" I demanded. "Why is there one in just about every single yard?"

"To honor him," Rolonda replied.

"Huh? Honor him?" I cried.

"You know what I mean," she said sharply. "People hope that if the evil snowman comes down from the ice cave, he'll see the little snowmen that look like him. It will make him happy and keep him from doing any harm."

Rolonda squeezed my hand. Her dark eyes burned into mine. "*Now* do you understand?" she whispered. "*Now* do you understand why we're all so afraid?"

I stared back at her — and burst out laughing.

17

I shouldn't have laughed. But I just couldn't help it.

I mean, Rolonda seemed like a really smart girl. She couldn't really believe that story — *could* she?

It's a joke, I decided. A story the villagers tell to scare people who move here.

I stopped laughing when I saw the startled expression on Rolonda's face. "Hey, come on," I said. "You're kidding — right?"

She shook her head solemnly. Her dark eyes glowed in the dim light. Such serious eyes.

"You don't really believe that a snowman can walk, do you?" I demanded. My voice echoed shrilly in the small room. "You don't really believe that a snowman can be alive!"

"I believe it," Rolonda replied in a low, trembling voice. "It's not a joke, Jaclyn. I believe it. And everyone in the village believes it."

I stared at her. The ceiling creaked, probably

59

from the weight of the snow on the roof. I shifted my weight on the hard wooden bench.

"But have you ever seen it?" I asked. "Have you ever seen the snowman walk?"

She blinked. "Well . . . no," she confessed. "But I've heard him late at night, Jaclyn. I've heard his howls and his angry cries."

She climbed to her feet. "I won't go close enough to see him. I'm too afraid," she said. "I won't go up to the ice cave. No one will."

"But, Rolonda —" I started.

Then I stopped. Her chin trembled. I could see the fear in her eyes.

Just *talking* about the snowman had frightened her.

I wanted to tell her that the story *couldn't* be true. I wanted to tell her that it sounded like a silly superstition. A fairy tale.

But I didn't want to insult her.

She might be my only friend here, I thought.

I stood up and pulled on my coat. Then the two of us made our way out of the church.

The snow had stopped. But a gusting wind blew down from the mountain. The wind made the fresh snow swirl and dance around our boots.

I pulled my hood over my hair and lowered my head into the wind. *No way* I could ever believe such a wild story, I thought. Why doesn't Rolonda see how crazy it is?

We made our way up the road, our boots sinking into the powdery, fresh snow. We didn't talk. Our voices wouldn't carry over the loud rush of the wind.

I walked Rolonda home. We stopped at the bottom of her snow-covered driveway. "Thanks for telling me about the snowman," I said.

Her eyes locked on mine. "You had to be told," she said solemnly. And then she added, "You've *got* to believe me, Jaclyn. It's true. All of it."

I didn't reply. I said good night. Then I turned and, leaning into the wind, headed for my house.

I was nearly there when I heard a sound over the roaring wind.

A heavy *THUD THUD THUD* coming up rapidly behind me.

18

I froze.

For a moment, I thought it was my imagination.

I pictured an enormous, evil snowman, as tall as a house, lumbering after me.

"No!" I murmured. And spun around. And saw Rolonda's brother, Eli, running up to me.

His heavy workboots thudded over the snow. His sheepskin coat was open, flapping out as he ran.

"Eli — it's late!" I cried. "What are you *doing* out here?"

He didn't reply. Breathing hard, his chest heaving up and down under his sweater, he eyed me suspiciously.

"She told you — didn't she?" he demanded breathlessly.

"Huh?" We moved behind a wide tree, out of the wind. "Eli — what is your problem?" I demanded.

"Rolonda told you — didn't she?" he repeated. "She told you about the snowman." He pointed toward the mountaintop.

"Well . . . yeah," I replied. A clump of snow dropped from the tree onto the front of my parka. I brushed it away.

"Eli, are you crazy? It's freezing out here! Zip up your coat," I scolded.

"Rolonda doesn't know one thing," Eli continued, still breathing hard. "She doesn't know that I saw it. I saw the snowman."

I stared at him. "You saw the snowman? You saw the living snowman?"

Eli nodded. "Yes. I saw him. But that's not the scary part."

"Eli — what *is* the scary part?" I demanded.

19

He stared at me. The wind ruffled his dark hair, but his eyes remained steady, hard.

"What is the scary part?" I repeated.

"The scary part," Eli replied, "is that the snowman saw *me*!"

The wind howled around the tree. I dragged Eli to the side of the nearest house. We pressed against the wall. Shivering, he finally zipped up his coat.

"Eli — the story is crazy," I insisted. "I really don't think —"

"Just let me tell you what happened," he pleaded. "Then you can decide if it's crazy or not."

He shivered again. "It saw me, Jaclyn. The snowman stared at me. It saw me. It knows who I am. It knows that I saw it. And that's why I'm so afraid of it."

"But, Eli —" I started.

He raised a gloved hand to silence me. "Wait. Please." He took a deep breath. "It happened a few weeks ago. My two friends and I — we climbed up the mountain. We wanted to see the ice cave. So we sneaked around Conrad's cabin."

"I don't get it," I said. "What does Conrad have to do with it?"

"He won't let anyone near the ice cave," Eli replied. "He keeps everyone away. Conrad is so weird. Some people think he works for the snowman. He protects the snowman by keeping everyone from the village away."

"But you sneaked past Conrad?" I asked.

Eli nodded. "Yeah. My friends and I. And we climbed up close to the ice cave. I had never seen the cave before."

"What does it look like?" I asked.

Eli made a sweeping motion with both hands, outlining the shape of the cave for me. "It's a huge cave, cut into the side of the mountain," he said. "It's made of ice. All smooth and shiny. It looks like glass.

"The cave entrance is wide and totally black. And it has huge icicles hanging down all along the front. With points as sharp as knives."

"Wow," I murmured. "It sounds kind of pretty."

"Yeah. In a way," Eli agreed. "But we didn't think it was pretty when the snowman came out."

I stared hard at Eli, studying his face. "You *really* saw a snowman walking?" I demanded.

Eli nodded. "We heard a rumbling sound. The

ground started to shake. My friends and I got scared. We thought it was an earthquake or an avalanche or something.

"My friends started to run down the mountain. But I stayed. And I saw it. The snowman poked his head out of the cave. He was as big as a grizzly bear. And he had a scar cut deep into his face.

"His eyes searched around. Then they stopped on me. And his mouth opened in an angry roar. He — he —"

Eli took a deep breath. Then he started again. "The snowman stepped out of the cave. The ground shook. It really did. Snow blew all over the place.

"The snowman stared at me. And he roared again. And — and I took off," Eli continued breathlessly. "I ran past Conrad's cabin. I ran all the way down the mountain. And I never looked back."

"What about your friends?" I asked.

"They were waiting for me down at the bottom," Eli replied. "We just went to our houses. We never talked about it."

"Why not?" I demanded.

"Too afraid, I guess," Eli said, glancing down. "We never talked about it. We never mentioned it. I never even told Rolonda. It was just too frightening to talk about."

He raised his eyes to me. "But now I have

66

dreams," he confessed. "Bad dreams about the snowman. Every night."

I stared at him, unsure of what to say. His whole body was trembling. From the cold? I wondered. Or from being so afraid?

He gazed back at me, waiting for me to say something. "Eli, you didn't tell Rolonda about this. Why are you telling me?" I asked.

"So you will believe the story," he replied solemnly. "You're new, Jaclyn. You probably think it's all silly. But you *have* to stay away from the ice cave."

"But, Eli —" I started.

"You didn't believe my sister — *did* you!" he accused. "You didn't believe her story."

"Well . . ." I hesitated.

"That's why I waited for you," he explained. "I waited to tell you *my* story. Do you believe *me*, Jaclyn? Do you believe that I saw the snowman?"

"I — I don't know," I told him.

The wind swirled around the wall of the house. I felt my nose and cheeks. My whole face was numb. "I've got to get home," I said.

Eli grabbed my parka sleeve. "Jaclyn, don't go up to the ice cave," he pleaded. "Please, believe my story. It's true."

I pulled my arm away. Then I started to jog over the snow toward my house. "Go home, Eli," I called back. "Go home before you freeze."

I jogged all the way home. It felt good to run and not think about anything.

Jogging on fresh, powdery snow was difficult. My boots kept slipping on the slick, hard surface underneath. By the time I reached home, my legs ached.

Breathing hard, I pushed open the front door. To my surprise, the house was totally dark.

I pulled off a glove and squinted at my wrist-watch. Only nine o'clock.

Did Aunt Greta go to bed so early? She usually stays up until at least midnight.

I clicked on the ceiling light and glanced around the small living room. A magazine lay open on the couch. Nothing else was out of place.

Leaning against the front door, I pulled off my wet boots and stood them in the corner. Then I tugged off my parka and dropped it onto the couch.

My eyes stopped at the door to Aunt Greta's bedroom.

The door stood open. Darkness beyond the door.

I quickly made my way across the room and peeked into my aunt's bedroom. "Aunt Greta?" I called softly.

No reply.

I stepped into the room. "Aunt Greta? Are you in here?"

I fumbled at the lamp on her dresser and finally managed to click it on.

"Aunt Greta — ?"

No. Not in bed. Not in her room.

"Aunt Greta — are you home?" I called loudly.

I headed out of her room. "Ohh!" I cried out when I stepped in something.

Something cold and wet soaked through my sock.

"Huh?" I lowered my gaze to see a wide puddle of cold water on the bedroom floor.

"How did *that* get there?" I murmured.

I suddenly felt worried.

"Aunt Greta?" I called, hurrying back into the living room. "Aunt Greta? Where *are* you?"

20

Panic swept over me.

Where could she be?

I started for the kitchen — when a rattling at the front door made me stop.

Was someone breaking in?

I gasped as the door slowly creaked open.

And Aunt Greta came bustling in, brushing snow off her long, black coat. She smiled at me. But her smile instantly died when she saw my expression.

"Jaclyn — what's wrong?"

"I — I — I —" I sputtered. "Aunt Greta — where *were* you? I got so scared."

She pulled off her coat. "Didn't you see my note?"

"Huh? Note?"

"I left it for you on the refrigerator," she said. "I met a nice couple this morning at the general store. They came by and invited me over for dessert and coffee."

"Oh. That's nice," I choked out. My heart still pounded in my chest.

"Why did you get scared?" Aunt Greta demanded, hanging her coat in the front closet. She straightened her long, white braid behind her sweater.

"Well, I was in your room. Looking for you. And I stepped in a cold puddle on the floor," I replied.

"Puddle? Show me," Aunt Greta demanded.

I led the way to the bedroom and pointed to the wide wet spot on the floor. Aunt Greta gazed up at the ceiling. "Maybe the roof leaks," she murmured. "We'll have to examine it tomorrow morning."

"I — I thought it was the snowman," I blurted out. "I know it's crazy, but I thought he had been here. I thought he'd broken into the house and —"

I stopped when I saw the shock on my aunt's face. Her mouth dropped open and she uttered a silent gasp.

"Jaclyn — what are you talking about?" she demanded. "What have your friends been telling you? More nonsense about a snowman?"

"Yes," I confessed. "Rolonda and Eli, the two village kids I met. They both told me a crazy story about a living snowman who stays in an ice cave at the top of the mountain. They said —"

"It's all superstition," Aunt Greta interrupted.

"It's all old tales that have been handed down. None of it is true. You're smart enough to know that, Jaclyn."

"Yes," I agreed. "But Rolonda and Eli seem so frightened. They really believe the story. And Eli begged me not to go up to the ice cave."

"Probably good advice," Aunt Greta said. She crossed the room and placed a hand tenderly on my shoulder. "You probably shouldn't go up to the mountaintop, dear," she said softly.

"Why not?" I demanded.

"There must be some kind of real danger up there," she replied. "Not a living snowman. But something else dangerous."

She sighed. "That's how these old stories get started. Something bad happened on the mountaintop. Then the story changed each time it was told. Years later, no one remembers what *really* happened. And now everyone believes a crazy story about a living snowman."

She shook her head.

"Have you seen all the strange snowmen in this village?" I asked her. "All the snowmen with scars on their faces and red scarves? Don't you think they're spooky?"

"It's a strange village tradition," Aunt Greta confessed. "Very quaint. I think they're very interesting looking."

"Interesting?" I frowned at her.

"Well, make me a promise," she said, yawning.

"Promise?"

"Promise me you won't go running up to the mountaintop to explore the ice cave. It probably is a very dangerous place."

"Well . . ." I hesitated.

"Promise," Aunt Greta urged sternly.

"Okay. I promise," I agreed, rolling my eyes.

But a few minutes later, I decided to break that promise.

I was lying in my attic bed, my eyes shut tight. Listening. Listening to the strange howls from the mountaintop.

Were they animal? Were they human?

I hate mysteries. I *have* to know the answers to things.

I'm going up there, I decided.

I don't care what I promised my aunt. I'm climbing up to the ice cave.

Tomorrow.

21

I didn't dream of snowmen that night. I dreamed about fluffy white kittens with sky-blue eyes. Dozens of them. The whitest kittens I ever saw.

They began climbing over one another. Silently at first. And then they started to screech and hiss. A frightening, ugly sound.

Suddenly they all wore red scarves around their necks.

They clawed at each other, arching their pure white backs. Hissing and screeching.

Until I woke up.

Yellow morning sunlight poured through the round window at the other end of my bedroom. I could smell bacon frying downstairs. Aunt Greta was already up and about.

I decided to climb the mountain right after breakfast. I didn't want to think about it anymore. I wanted to go up there and solve the mystery.

I knew that strange, white-bearded guy Conrad was a problem. If he saw me, he'd try to stop me. He and his wolf.

But I had a plan to take care of Conrad.

If only Rolonda and Eli would help . . .

As it turned out, I didn't get out of the house till after lunch. Aunt Greta needed me to hang curtains with her. And then we put up the paintings and posters she had brought from Chicago.

The house was tiny and cramped. But it was starting to feel a little more like home.

"Where are you going?" Aunt Greta called as I pulled on my parka and gloves and started out the door.

"Uh . . . nowhere really," I lied. "Just going to hang out with Rolonda and Eli."

As I said their names, I saw them walking up my front yard.

I closed the front door behind me and hurried out to greet them. Eli carried a snow shovel. Rolonda dragged two slender tree branches. She dropped them at my feet.

"What's that for?" I asked. "What are you guys doing here?"

"We have to build your snowman," Rolonda replied solemnly.

"Excuse me?" I cried.

"You won't be safe until you have a snowman in your yard," Eli said.

"Listen, guys . . ." I started.

"The snow is very wet," Rolonda reported.

"Good packing snow. It shouldn't take long. Eli and I brought everything we need."

"But I don't have time to build a snowman," I protested. "I want to climb up to the ice cave this morning."

They both gasped. Eli gripped the shovel handle and gaped at me.

"You can't — !" Eli cried.

"Jaclyn, I warned you —" Rolonda said.

"I have to see it for myself," I told them. And then I added, "I want you to come with me."

"No!" Eli gasped.

Rolonda just shook her head. "You know we won't go up to the ice cave, Jaclyn. And we don't want you to go, either."

"But if we all go together . . ." I urged.

"No!" they both cried.

I could see real fear on their faces. Staring at them, I suddenly had an idea.

"Okay, okay," I said. "I'll make a deal with you."

They eyed me suspiciously. "What kind of deal?" Rolonda demanded.

"I'll stay here and build the snowman — if you will help me when we're done," I said.

"No. We won't go with you," Rolonda insisted. "You can't get us to go up to the ice cave, Jaclyn."

"No deal," Eli added sternly.

"You don't have to go up to the ice cave," I told

them. "You just have to keep Conrad busy so I can sneak past him."

"Huh? How are we going to do that?" Eli asked, leaning on the shovel.

"We'll think of something when we get up there," I replied. "If you can keep him talking to you, maybe I can sneak past and get up to the cave."

"But we don't *want* you to go to the ice cave!" Rolonda insisted.

"I'm going to do it one way or the other," I told her. "With or without you. So are you going to help me or not?"

They glanced tensely at each other. Eli whispered something to his sister. Rolonda whispered something back.

Then Rolonda turned to me. "Will you build the snowman first?" she asked.

"You won't be safe without the snowman," Eli added.

I wanted to tell them that building a snowman wouldn't protect me against anything. I wanted to tell them how silly the whole thing was.

But I needed their help. I knew I could never get past Conrad and his wolf without them.

"Okay. Fine. First, we'll build the snowman," I agreed.

"Then Eli and I will help you," Rolonda promised.

"But we won't go any farther than Conrad's cabin," Eli insisted in a trembling voice.

"Great!" I replied. "Let's get started."

I bent down and started rolling a snowball for the snowman's body. Rolonda was right. It was good packing snow. I rolled the ball across my snowy yard until it was big enough for two of us to roll. Rolonda and I worked on the body. Eli worked on the snowball for the head.

Building one of the strange snowmen gave me a creepy feeling. I felt as if I had become part of the superstition. I was taking part in some kind of ancient village tradition. A tradition built on fear.

The people of the village all built these snowmen because they were afraid. And now here I was, building one, too.

Should I be afraid? I wondered.

I felt glad when the snowman was finished. Rolonda pulled a red scarf from her coat pocket, and we wrapped it under the scarred head.

The snowman's dark eyes seemed to glare at me. The mouth was turned down in an angry sneer. The arms bobbed softly in the wind.

"Okay. Good job," I told my two new friends. "Now let's get going." I motioned toward the mountaintop.

"Are you sure you want to do this?" Eli asked in a tiny voice.

"Sure, I'm sure!" I declared loudly.

But as we started making our way along the road, I didn't feel as sure as I pretended.

The road curved up the mountain. Soon the houses ended and we were walking through snowy woods.

We didn't talk. We kept our eyes straight ahead.

The afternoon sun was slowly lowering itself behind the trees. Blue shadows stretched over the snow. The air grew colder as we climbed.

When Conrad's low cabin came into view, my heart began to pound.

I tried to keep my mind calm and clear. But question after question whirred through my brain.

Was Conrad inside the cabin?

Where was the white wolf?

Would my plan work?

22

All three of us stopped at the end of the road and stared at the cabin up ahead. The late afternoon sun had fallen behind the trees. The snow billowed in front of us in shades of gray.

To the left of the cabin, I saw a row of low evergreen shrubs, covered in snow.

"I'll hide behind those shrubs," I told Rolonda and Eli. "You run up to the cabin and keep Conrad and the wolf from seeing me."

"This isn't going to work," Eli muttered, his eyes on the cabin.

"It's getting kind of dark," Rolonda fretted. "Maybe we should come back in the morning."

"Maybe we should forget the whole idea," Eli suggested. I saw his chin quiver. He shuddered.

"Hey — you promised!" I exclaimed. "A promise is a promise — right?"

They didn't reply. They both stared across the gray snow at the dark cabin up ahead.

"I came this far. I'm not going back," I said sharply. "Are you going to help me or not?"

I gasped when I heard a low growl from the cabin. The wolf must have heard or smelled us.

I knew it would come running out any second.

"Come *on*!" I urged in a loud whisper. And I took off for the snow-covered shrubs.

I ducked out of view just as Conrad and the wolf burst out of the cabin.

"Hello!" Rolonda cried to Conrad.

"Hi!" Eli echoed.

I watched Rolonda and Eli go running up to Conrad.

The wolf lowered its head, watching them carefully.

I saw Rolonda and Eli, both talking at once, chattering with Conrad. I couldn't hear what they were saying.

They're doing it! I told myself, my heart pounding. They're keeping his attention.

Time for me to move.

Time for me to make a run for it.

I could hear Rolonda talking to Conrad. I glanced over the top of the bush. The wolf had its back to me.

Conrad was scratching his gray hair, listening to Rolonda. I couldn't see his expression. But I imagined he was very confused and surprised.

I knew he didn't get any visitors.

He must be wondering what Rolonda and Eli were doing up here!

I forced all of these thoughts from my mind.

It was time for me to make a run for it.

I took a deep breath.

Then, still crouching, I began to run.

My legs felt like Jell-O. My boots sank into the deep snow.

Ducking my head, I darted up the steep mountain side.

Up, up.

I had just passed the bushes when I heard Conrad's angry shout — "Hey, *wait!*"

23

I stopped so suddenly, I fell over backward!

I landed hard. The snow seemed to fly up in my face, sweep over me, surround me. Everything went white.

I'm caught, I realized.

My plan didn't work.

I stood up and turned to face Conrad.

To my shock, he wasn't coming after me. He and the wolf were running downhill. Chasing after Rolonda and Eli.

I heard the wolf utter a high growl. Then they disappeared around a curve.

I stood frozen in place, staring at the spot where they had just been.

Would Conrad harm Rolonda and Eli?

Should I run after them and try to help them?

No. I had to keep going.

This was the plan. This was my chance.

Taking another deep breath, I turned and started to run up the mountainside. The climb was steep for a while. So steep I wasn't sure I could make it.

But then the ground leveled off. I found myself on a wide ledge. The ledge was slick. My boots slipped on the ice.

I pressed my back against the mountain wall.

And gazed up at the ice cave.

Yes!

There it stood above me. A cave as tall as a building. Smooth and glassy, it reflected the clouds in the sky above it.

I couldn't see the entrance from here. I was staring at one of the sides.

The ledge narrowed as it curled up to the cave.

I kept my back pressed against the wall and slowly — step by step — inched my way toward the top.

"Don't look down!" I murmured out loud.

But as soon as I said it, I had to look.

It was a deep drop from the ledge to the ground far, far below.

If I slipped and fell . . .

I'm not going to slip and fall! I told myself.

A deep, rumbling sound made me jump!

I grabbed the mountainside with both hands to keep from falling.

The ledge trembled beneath me.

Another low rumble made me cry out in fear.

The ledge trembled again. The whole mountain seemed to shake!

The sound came from the cave.

Is something moving up there? I wondered.

Or is it the normal sound of a mountaintop in the wind?

I gathered my courage and moved forward. Inch by inch.

I had come this far. I refused to retreat now.

The ledge grew narrower, slipperier, as it curved around.

Another rumbling noise made me gasp.

Somehow I held on. And followed the ledge around.

It seemed to take forever. But then the cave opening came into view.

And after that, I saw the most terrifying sight of my life.

24

I didn't see it at first.

First, I saw the layer of solid ice that covered the ledge. The glassy cave rose up behind the ledge. The gaping entrance to the cave was blacker than the darkest night.

I stood staring into the darkness. Trying to catch my breath. Trying to slow my pounding heart.

Clouds reflected in the glassy ice drifted rapidly to the right. They made the cave appear to move.

Sharply pointed icicles stabbed down from the roof of the cave opening. They reminded me of sharpened teeth about to close.

I stared into the black cave opening and waited. Waited to see if anything would appear.

I didn't have to wait long.

A rumble as loud as thunder made the ledge quake.

Afraid I might slip off, I dropped to my knees.

The rumble grew to a roar.

And a tall, white figure lumbered out from the blackness of the cave entrance. An enormous snowman!

I gasped — and stared in horror as the mountain of snow moved toward me. "Nooooo!" I wailed.

I forgot where I was. Forgot I was perched on a narrow ice ledge.

And started to back up, to back away from the tall creature.

And I slipped.

Slipped off the ledge.

And felt myself fall.

25

My hands shot up.

Shot up and dug into the ledge.

I gripped the icy ledge. Held on. Held on.

With a terrified groan, I scrambled back up to safety. Trembling. My entire body shaking. My breaths escaping in short, frantic gasps.

I huddled on my knees on the icy ledge and watched the snowman as it glared down at me. Its blood-red scarf flapped in the wind. Its round, black eyes were as big as doorknobs. Its dark mouth turned down in a fierce, angry sneer.

And the scar. The scar cut deeply into the side of its round head, long and curling, like a black snake.

"Ohhhhhh." I uttered another moan as its tree branch arms reached for me.

I shivered in a sudden, deep cold. A cold I'd never felt before. I could see frozen waves floating from the snowman's wide body.

And then the big, round head tilted. The black eyes bulged even wider.

And the snowman bellowed in a deep roar of a voice: "*WHO ARE YOU?*"

I trembled in the waves of cold that floated off its body.

It talks!

The stories Rolonda and Eli told me are true. It's all true.

Its round eyes locked on mine, the big snowman moved closer. Closer.

I wanted to stand up. I wanted to run.

But it had me frozen there.

I couldn't stand. I couldn't back up. I couldn't escape from it.

"*WHO ARE YOU?*" the snowman bellowed again. And the whole mountain shook.

"I — I —" My voice came out in a quivering squeak.

"Please —" I managed to choke out. "Please — I didn't mean to bother you. I —"

"*WHO ARE YOU?*" the huge snow creature thundered for the third time.

"My name?" I squeaked. "My name is Jaclyn. Jaclyn DeForest."

The snowman's tree branch arms shot up. Its dark mouth gaped open in surprise.

"*SAY IT AGAIN,*" it ordered.

I shivered in the waves of cold. "Jaclyn DeForest," I repeated in my tiny, frightened voice.

The snowman stared down at me in silence for a long while. It lowered its arms to its round, white sides.

"*DO YOU KNOW WHO I AM?*" it demanded.

I swallowed hard. The question took me totally by surprise. I opened my mouth to answer, but no sound came out.

"*DO YOU KNOW WHO I AM?*" the snowman thundered.

"No," I squeaked. "Who are you?"

"*I AM YOUR FATHER!*" the snowman cried.

26

"Nooooooo!" A long wail escaped my throat.

I wanted to get away from there. I wanted to run. To slide down the mountain. To *fly* away.

But I couldn't move.

The snowman trapped me in his icy grip. Held me there on the ledge. Froze me in wave after wave of cold.

"Jaclyn — I am your father," the snowman repeated, lowering his booming voice. He stared down at me with those frightening, round glassy eyes. "Believe me."

"Th-that's *impossible*!" I stammered. I hugged myself, trying to stop my body from trembling. "You're a snowman! You *can't* be my father!"

"Listen to me!" the snowman roared. "I am your father. Your mother was a sorceress. And so is your aunt. Your aunt practices all sorts of magic."

"No — !" I protested. His lies made me gather my courage. I climbed to my feet.

"That's not true!" I cried angrily. "I've never seen Aunt Greta do any magic. You're lying!"

The snowman bobbed from side to side. The ledge shook beneath me. I nearly lost my balance.

"I do not lie, Jaclyn," he insisted. His arms raised up, as if he were pleading with me. "I'm telling the truth."

"But — but —" I sputtered.

"Your mother did this to me," the snowman said. "She used her magic and turned me into a snowman. You were two years old. She turned me into a snowman. She tried to turn me back. But she failed. Then she and your aunt Greta took you and ran away from the village."

"Your story doesn't make any sense!" I cried. "If what you say is true, why did we move back here? Why did Aunt Greta bring us back to the village?"

"Your aunt had a good reason for coming back," the snowman explained. "She knows that after ten years, the magic spell starts to fade."

"I — I don't understand," I stammered. My head felt frozen. It was hard to think. I struggled to make sense of what he was telling me.

"After ten years, the spell fades," the snowman repeated. "Your aunt came back to renew the spell. She wants me to stay a snowman. She wants to keep me prisoner up here forever. She wants to make sure I don't tell the world what happened to me. And she wants to keep you to herself!"

"Aunt Greta is *not* a sorceress!" I protested. "I've lived with her most of my life. And I've never seen her do any kind of magic. She doesn't —"

"PLEASE!" the snowman bellowed, raising a tree branch arm to silence me. "There isn't much time. I'm your father, Jaclyn. Your real father. You've *got* to believe me."

"But, I — I —" I didn't know what to say. I couldn't think straight. It was all too . . . crazy.

"You can get me out of this," the snowman pleaded. "You can save me. But you've got to hurry. Your aunt Greta will renew the spell soon. If you don't save me, I'll be a snowman for another ten years."

"But what can I do?" I cried. "I'm not a sorceress. I can't do magic. What can I do?"

"You can save me," the giant snow creature insisted. "But I cannot tell you how." He uttered a bitter sigh.

"If I tell you how to save me, it will only *strengthen* the spell," he continued. "You've got to figure it out for yourself."

"Huh? But how?" I demanded.

"I can give you a hint," the snowman replied. "I cannot tell you how to save me. But I can give you a hint."

"Okay," I said softly. I hugged myself more tightly.

And I listened as, in his deep rumble of a voice, the snowman recited the familiar rhyme:

"When the snows blow wild
And the day grows old,
Beware, the snowman, my child.
Beware, the snowman.
He brings the cold."

I stared up at him in shock. "You — you know the poem!" I stammered.

"That is your clue," the snowman said softly. "That is the only hint I can give you. Now you must figure out how to rescue me."

I already knew how to rescue him.

I knew instantly when he recited the old rhyme.

The *second verse*. The secret had to be in the second verse. The verse I couldn't remember.

"Please, Jaclyn." The snowman gazed down at me, pleading. "Please. Help me. I'm your father, Jaclyn. I'm really your father."

I stared back at him. Trying to decide. Trying so hard to decide.

Should I believe him?

Should I help him?

94

27

Yes, I decided.

Yes. I'll run home. I'll find the old poetry book. And I'll read the second verse of the rhyme.

"I'm coming back!" I called up to the snowman. I spun away from him, pulled myself out of his invisible, cold grip.

I started to run down the ledge. And gasped when I nearly ran into Aunt Greta!

"Aunt Greta — !" I cried in shock.

"I tried to warn you!" she called to me. "I tried to scare you, Jaclyn. To keep you from coming up here."

So, it was Aunt Greta who whispered up to my room late at night, who warned me to beware of the snowman!

Her dark eyes were wild. Her normally pale face was bright red! Her long, black coat was open and flapped behind her in the wind.

She raised a large, black book in one hand

above her head. "Jaclyn — is *this* what you're looking for?" she demanded shrilly.

"The poetry book?" I cried.

My aunt nodded. She held the book high above her.

"Aunt Greta — is it true?" I asked, glancing back at the huge snowman. "Is he really my father?"

My aunt's face twisted in surprise. "Huh? Your father?" she cried. "What a lie! Is *that* what he told you? That he's your father? It's a lie. A horrible lie!"

"NOOOOOO!" the snowman boomed.

I jumped. But Aunt Greta ignored the thunderous cry.

"It's a lie, Jaclyn," she repeated, glaring angrily at the snowman. "He isn't your father. He's an evil monster!"

"NOOOOO!" the snowman bellowed again. The whole mountain shook from his protest.

"Your mother and father were sorcerers," Aunt Greta continued, ignoring him. "They practiced their magic night and day. But they went too far. They created him accidentally."

Aunt Greta pointed to the snowman, her face bitter. "He's an evil monster," she repeated through gritted teeth. "When your parents saw what they had done, they were horrified. They froze the monster inside the snowman body. Soon after, your father disappeared. Your mother and

I took you and ran from the village. We ran to be safe from the monster's horrible evil!"

"YOU ARE A LIAR!" the snowman raged. He waved his stick arms wildly in the air. His scarf blew out at his sides like hawk wings. Wave after wave of cold shot off his bulging body.

"Jaclyn, don't believe her!" the snowman pleaded. "Save me — please! I am your father."

His arms reached out to me. "Please," he begged. "I know it is hard for you to believe. But your aunt is the evil one. She is a sorceress. She and your mother and I — we were all sorcerers. I am not evil. I am not a monster. Please —"

"Liar!" Aunt Greta shrieked. She gripped the big book angrily in both hands, as if ready to throw it at him. "I know no magic!" Aunt Greta cried. "I know no spells! I am not a sorceress!"

She opened the book and began frantically shuffling through the pages. "I'm not a sorceress. But I brought this book because I know its secret. I know what I need to do to make sure you stay frozen in that snowman body forever!"

The snowman continued to reach out to me. "Jaclyn, save me. Save me now," he pleaded.

I turned from him to my aunt, then back to him.

Who should I believe?

Which one was telling the truth?

Suddenly, I had an idea.

28

I grabbed the open poetry book from my aunt's hands.

"What are you *doing*?" she shrieked.

She moved quickly to wrestle it away from me.

We both tugged at it. The old pages tore and flew out. The heavy cover cracked.

Aunt Greta made a desperate swipe at it.

But I pulled it away from her. Then I backed up against the wall of the ice cave.

Aunt Greta took a step toward me. Then she gazed up at the snowman and decided not to come that close to him.

"Jaclyn — you're making a big mistake!" Aunt Greta warned.

Leaning against the smooth cave wall, I flipped frantically through the pages of the old book. "I'm going to find the poem," I told her. "I'm going to read the second verse. It's the only way to know the truth."

"THANK YOU, DAUGHTER!" the snowman bellowed.

Aunt Greta uttered a wail of protest. "I'm telling you the truth, Jaclyn!" she cried. "I have taken care of you all these years. I would not lie to you."

But I'd made up my mind.

I had to read the second verse. It was the only way I could find out who was lying and who was telling the truth.

"He's a monster!" Aunt Greta cried.

The snowman stood still and silent, watching me furiously shuffle through the pages.

Where was that rhyme? Where?

I glanced up. "Aunt Greta — ?"

She bent down and picked up a torn page from the snow. As her eyes moved over the page, a smile spread over her face.

The wind blew her coat behind her. Her eyes were wild. The page fluttered in her hand.

"Jaclyn, I can't let you read the rhyme," she said.

"You — you have it in your hand?" I cried.

"I can't let you read it," Aunt Greta repeated.

And tossed the page over the ledge.

29

I let out a shriek.

I watched the page float out over the ledge. I watched it fly up, then start to drop.

It's lost, I realized.

The second verse is lost forever.

The swirling wind will carry it down the mountain, down the steep drop. It will never be seen again.

And then, I cried out again — as the wind carried the page up. Up. Back up.

And into my hand!

I grabbed it out of the air.

I stared at it in amazement.

And before Aunt Greta could grab it back, I raised the page to my face and started to read the second verse of the rhyme out loud:

"When the snows melt
And the warm sun is with thee,
Beware, the snowman —"

"Noooooo!" Aunt Greta wailed. She dove toward me. With a desperate swipe, she pulled the page from my hand.

And ripped it to shreds.

The snowman uttered a horrified groan. He bent. Reached out to grab Aunt Greta.

Too late.

The jagged strips of paper fluttered to the snow.

"Aunt Greta — why?" I choked out.

"I couldn't let you do it," she replied. "He's a monster, Jaclyn. He's not your father. I couldn't let you free him."

"She's lying," the snowman insisted. "She does not want you to know me, Jaclyn. She doesn't want you to know your own father. She wants to leave me trapped in this frozen cave forever."

I turned back to my aunt. Her face had grown stern and hard. She stared back at me coldly.

I took a deep breath. "Aunt Greta, I have to know the truth," I told her.

"I've told you the truth," she insisted.

"I have to know for myself," I replied. "I — I saw the last line of the poem. Before you grabbed it and tore it up. I know the whole poem, Aunt Greta."

"Don't —" my aunt pleaded, reaching out to me.

But I backed up against the icy cave wall, and I recited the rhyme from memory:

101

"When the snows melt
And the warm sun is with thee,
Beware, the snowman —
For the snowman shall go free!"

"No, Jaclyn! No! No! No!" Aunt Greta wailed. She pressed her hands to the sides of her face and repeated her cry. "No! No! No!"

I turned to the snowman and saw him begin to melt.

The white snow oozed down his face and body like melting ice cream.

The black eyes dropped to the snow. The face melted, melted onto the body. The snow poured off the round body. The tree branch arms thudded heavily to the ground.

Slowly his real face came into view.

Slowly his body emerged from under the snow.

I stared as the snow dripped away.

And then I opened my mouth in a shrill scream of horror.

30

A monster!

An ugly, snarling, red-skinned monster stomped out from under the oozing snow.

Aunt Greta had told the truth. A monster was trapped inside the snowman. Not my father.

Not my father.

A monster . . . such a hideous monster!

Its head and body were covered with crusty red scales. Its yellow eyes rolled wildly in its bull-shaped head. A purple tongue flapped from its jagged-toothed mouth.

"No! No! No! No!" Aunt Greta chanted, still pressing both hands against her face. Tears ran down her cheeks and over her hands.

"What have I done?" I wailed.

The monster tossed back its head in a throaty laugh. He picked the poetry book off the snow in his scaly, three-fingered hands. And he heaved it over the side of the mountain.

"You're next!" he roared at me.

"No — please!" I begged.

I grabbed Aunt Greta by the shoulders and tugged her away from the ledge. We pressed ourselves against the icy wall of the cave.

"Good-bye," the monster grunted. "Good-bye, all."

"But I *saved* you!" I pleaded. "Is that my reward? To be thrown over the side of the mountain?"

The red-scaled beast nodded. An ugly grin revealed more jagged teeth. "Yes. That is your reward."

He picked me up in one powerful hand. Squeezing my waist. Squeezing it so tightly I couldn't breathe.

He picked Aunt Greta up in his other hand.

Raised us above his head.

Let out an ugly, raspy groan.

And held us over the side of the mountain.

31

His powerful hands swung us out over the cliff edge.

I peered down, down at the sheer drop, at the snowy ground that appeared to be miles below.

To my surprise, the monster didn't let go.

He swung around and dropped my aunt and me back onto the ledge.

"Huh?" I uttered a startled gasp.

The monster was staring down the ledge now. He had stopped paying attention to Aunt Greta and me.

Struggling to catch my breath, I turned and followed his gaze.

And saw what had startled the monster. And saved my life.

A parade!

A parade of snowmen.

All of the snowmen of the village. They were marching up to the ice cave in a single line.

Their red scarves waved in the wind. Their

sticklike arms bobbed up and down as they rumbled up the mountainside.

Like soldiers, they came marching up to us. Bouncing, thudding, rumbling forward. All identical. All scarred and stern-faced and sneering.

"I — I don't believe it!" I stammered. I grabbed Aunt Greta's arm.

We stared at the marching snowmen in horror.

"They're all coming to serve the monster," Aunt Greta whispered. "We're doomed, Jaclyn. Doomed."

32

The snowmen rumbled up the icy ledge. The steady *thud thud thud* grew louder as they neared. The sound echoed off the snowy mountaintop until it sounded as if a *thousand* snowmen were marching to attack us.

Aunt Greta and I shrank back against the glassy cave wall.

We had nowhere to run. The monster blocked the cave entrance. The marching snowmen cut off any escape down the ledge.

Closer came the snowmen. Closer. Close enough to see the anger in their round, black eyes. Close enough to see the snakelike scars cut into their faces.

Aunt Greta and I couldn't move. We raised our hands as if to shield ourselves.

And then we gasped in surprise as the snowmen marched right past us.

They rumbled up to the monster. Bouncing

fast. Thudding over the ice. Arms waving, dark eyes glowing.

Bounced up to the startled monster. And pushed him. Pushed him back.

The snowmen crushed up against him. One snowman. Then two. Then ten.

They crushed against his scaly, red body. Pushing him back. Back.

The monster tossed its head in an angry roar.

But the roar was smothered as a snowman rolled over the monster's head.

Aunt Greta and I gasped in amazement as the snowmen swarmed over the monster.

Pushed him back against the cave wall.

We saw the monster's powerful arms flail the air, thrashing wildly. Helplessly.

And then the monster disappeared behind a crush of snowmen.

The snowmen pushed forward. Pushed hard. Pushed silently.

Like a silent avalanche.

And when they finally stepped back, the monster stood frozen, arms stretched out as if to attack. Not moving. Frozen inside the ice wall.

A prisoner.

The snowmen had pushed him into the wall. Trapped him inside the glassy wall of ice.

Aunt Greta and I stood trembling beside the cave entrance. We were still holding on to each other. My legs felt weak and rubbery. I could feel Aunt Greta trembling beneath her coat.

"What brought all the snowmen up here?" I asked her. "Did *you* do it, Aunt Greta?"

She shook her head, her eyes still wide with amazement. "I didn't bring them here, Jaclyn," she said softly. "I told you the truth. I have no magic. Your mother and father were sorcerers. But not me."

"Then *who* made them climb the mountain to rescue us?" I demanded.

"I did!" a voice cried.

33

I turned to the ledge — and saw Conrad standing there. His gray hair blew wildly in the wind. The white wolf stood at his side.

"You made the snowmen march?" I cried. "You are a sorcerer, too?"

Conrad nodded. He gazed at the monster trapped in the ice and a smile spread over his face. "Yes. I sent them to rescue you," he said.

Aunt Greta narrowed her eyes at Conrad. As she studied his face, her mouth dropped open. "You!" Aunt Greta cried. "It's you!"

Conrad's smile grew even wider. "Yes," he told my aunt.

"Who — who is he?" I demanded.

Aunt Greta turned to me and placed a hand on my shoulder. "Jaclyn," she said softly, "I moved back here because I thought he might still be here. And yes, I was right. He *is* here."

She squeezed my shoulder and smiled at me,

tears welling in her eyes. "Conrad is your father," Aunt Greta whispered.

Conrad and I both cried out at the same time.

He rushed across the icy ledge and wrapped me in a hug. His long beard scratched my face as he pressed his cheek against mine.

"I don't believe it!" he cried, stepping back with tears in his eyes. "It's been so many years — I didn't recognize you, Jaclyn. I'm so glad that Greta brought you back to the village."

"You — you're *really* my father?" I stammered.

Conrad didn't have a chance to answer. Rolonda and Eli came running up to us. "Are you okay?" they cried.

Conrad pointed to Rolonda and Eli. "They saved your lives!" he told Aunt Greta and me. "They told me that you planned to climb to the ice cave. As soon as I heard that, I worked my magic. I sent the snowmen up to rescue you."

"Wow!" Eli exclaimed, seeing the monster frozen in the ice. "Look at that!"

"That was the evil snowman," Conrad explained to them. "He'll never threaten the village again."

Rolonda and Eli stepped closer to view the frozen monster close up.

I turned to my father. "I don't understand," I said. "Why did you stay behind in the village when Mom and Aunt Greta left? Why do you live up here near the ice cave?"

He scratched his beard and sighed. "It's kind of a long story. When you were little, your mother and I were practicing powerful magic. Our magic got out of control. We accidentally created this monster."

He motioned to the monster and shook his head. "We froze the monster inside the body of a snowman," he explained. "Your mother — she wanted to leave. She was so frightened and upset. She wanted to move as far away from the village as she could. She wanted to forget it ever happened."

"And why did you stay?" I demanded.

"I stayed because I thought I owed it to the people of the village," he explained. "I owed it to them to keep the snowman in his cave. To keep him from harming people."

He uttered another sad sigh. "And so I stayed up here, close to the monster we created. But . . . but . . . leaving you, Jaclyn, was the hardest thing I ever had to do!"

He wrapped his arm around my shoulders. Again, his beard scratched my face.

"I always dreamed that someday I could leave the mountain and go find you," he said softly. "And now the monster is dead. The horror is finally over. And Greta has brought you back. Perhaps . . ."

His voice broke. He smiled at Aunt Greta and then at me. He took a breath and tried again. "Perhaps . . . we can try to be a family again."

He kept his arm around me as we turned to go down the mountain.

"Hey — !" I cried out as I saw the snowmen move to block our path.

In all the excitement of finding my father, I'd completely forgotten about all the snowmen!

Now they circled us. Surrounded us.

Staring at us with their glowing coal eyes. Staring at us so coldly.

"Wh-what are they going to do?" I stammered.

Before my father could answer, one of the snowmen came thumping out of the group. He rumbled up to us, arms twitching, eyes flashing.

I grabbed Dad's arm. The snowmen had us totally surrounded.

Nowhere to move. No chance to run away.

The snowman stopped inches from my father — and opened his mouth to speak.

"Can we go back down now?" the snowman asked. "It's really *cold* up here!"

About the Author

R.L. Stine is the most popular author in America. He is the creator of the *Goosebumps*, *Give Yourself Goosebumps*, *Fear Street*, and *Ghosts of Fear Street* series, among other popular books. He has written more than 100 scary novels for kids. Bob lives in New York City with his wife, Jane, teenage son, Matt, and dog, Nadine.

Add *more*

Goosebumps®

to your collection . . .
A chilling preview of
what's next from
R.L. STINE

HOW I LEARNED TO FLY

"Wow! Morty! I can fly!"

Morty cocked his furry head at me.

"I know it sounds weird, boy. But it says so right here!" I pointed to the page I was reading. "Humans can fly!"

Wait a minute. Am I crazy? Have I totally lost it? People cannot fly.

Morty jumped up on a kitchen chair. He stared down at the book. At a picture of a young girl. With arms stretched out to her sides, she sailed through the air — her long, blond hair flowing behind her.

Morty glanced up at me. Peered back down at the page. Then he whimpered and bolted from the room.

"Come back, Morty. Don't you want to learn to fly?" I laughed. "Morty — The First and Only Flying Dog!"

I turned back to the book and read:

"For as long as humans have walked the earth,

they have yearned to fly. To float like an angel. To glide like a bat. To soar like a mighty bird of prey.

"All a dream. A hopeless dream — until now.

"The ancient secret of human flight is a simple one.

"You need only three things: the daring to try, an imagination that soars, and a good mixing bowl."

Hey —! I stared at the page. I had those things. Maybe I should give it a try. I had nothing better to do today.

I read on.

There, on the next page, the book told *exactly* what you needed to do to fly.

It gave some exercises to practice. And a magical mixture you had to eat.

Learn the Motion, Eat the Potion — that's what it said.

Finally it gave an ancient chant to recite.

And that was it. The secret of flying — right there.

Yeah, right. I rolled my eyes.

I scanned the list of ingredients I would need to make the potion. The main ingredient was yeast — "because yeast rises."

Hmmm. Yeast *does* rise. Maybe this really would work. Maybe I really could learn to fly.

If I could — it would be awesome. I would soar through the sky — just like my superheros.

I could fly, I thought dreamily as I searched

the pantry for the yeast. *Something Wilson couldn't do in a million years!*

And, boy, would Mia be impressed.

I could hear her now. "Oh, wow! Oh, wow! Oh, wow!" she would scream as I flew into the sky, leaving Wilson down on the ground — like a bug.

I'm going to do it right now! I'm going to learn how to fly!

Of course I knew it was crazy. But what if it worked? What if it really worked?

I turned to the page with the exercises. "Step One," I read out loud. "Hold your arms straight out in front of you. Bend your knees slightly. Now take fifty little hops in this position."

I did it. I felt like an idiot, but I did it.

"Step Two. Sit on the floor. Place your left foot on your right shoulder. Then lift your right leg and tuck it behind your head."

This was harder to do. A lot harder. I tugged my left foot up until it reached my shoulder. A sharp pain shot down my side. But I wasn't giving up.

I lifted my right leg up, up, up to my chin — then I lost my balance and rolled onto my back!

I tried it again. This time I rolled to the side.

Learning to fly wasn't going to be as easy as I thought.

I tried one more time — and got it.

But now I was stuck — all twisted up. My left foot perched on my right shoulder, with my toes jammed in my ears. My other foot pressed against the back of my head — shoving my face into my chest.

I struggled to untangle myself.

I stopped struggling when I heard someone laugh.

And realized I wasn't alone.

9

"What . . . are . . . you . . . doing?"

"Ray, is that you?" I tried to look up, but I couldn't. My chin was slammed tight against my chest.

"Yes, it's me. Ethan is here, too. *What* are you doing?" he repeated.

"He must be practicing for Twister," Ethan suggested.

They both laughed.

"Very funny, guys," I said. "Can you pull me apart? I think I'm stuck."

Ray and Ethan untangled me. "Whoa, that feels better," I said, stretching out my arms and legs.

"So — what *were* you doing?" Ethan asked the question this time.

"Exercising," I mumbled. "I was exercising. To . . . uh . . . improve my tennis game."

"Whoa. Those were pretty weird exercises." Ethan's eyebrows arched way up.

"He wasn't exercising for tennis!" Ray exclaimed. "He doesn't even play tennis!"

"I'm thinking of taking it up," I said quickly.

Ray narrowed his eyes at me. He didn't believe me. But he didn't ask any more questions.

"Want to shoot some hoops in the playground?" Ethan asked.

I didn't want to go anywhere.

I wanted to stay home. Alone. And see if I could fly.

"No, I have to stay home with Morty," I lied. "He's not feeling well."

Morty heard his name and charged full speed into the kitchen. He leaped on Ray and licked his face.

"He looks okay to me," Ray said, narrowing his eyes at me again.

"No problem. We can stay here," Ethan suggested. "Toss a football around or something."

Ethan glanced around the kitchen. His eyes fell on the book.

"No. Sorry. I really can't hang out," I said, tossing the book in the trash can. "I have to clean up the kitchen." I turned to the counter and wiped it with a sponge. Then I began lining up the spices in the spice rack — labels facing out.

"And I have to stay inside anyway. To wait for Mom and Dad to call. They're away. They said to sit by the phone."

"Why?" Ethan asked. "What's so important?"

"They wouldn't tell me. They said it's a surprise." I shrugged my shoulders.

"Okay, see you later — maybe," Ray said. Both guys were shaking their heads as they left.

I grabbed the book out of the garbage and flipped back to the exercise page.

I read the flapping and leaping exercises next. I did them all.

Now it was time to say the magic words.

I read them to myself first. To make sure I got them right. Then I recited them out loud, slowly.

Hishram hishmar shah shahrom shom.

I climbed up on the kitchen chair — and jumped off. To see if I felt different. Lighter. Floaty.

I landed with a hard *thud.*

Guess I need to eat the special flying food for the full effect, I decided. I turned back to the book.

It was time to start mixing.

In a cabinet next to the refrigerator, I found our good mixing bowl. I dumped all the ingredients into it: 10 egg yolks, 1 tablespoon of maple syrup, 2 cups of flour, 1/2 cup of seltzer, and 4 tablespoons of yeast.

I stirred. A lumpy yellow blob of dough started to form.

I turned the page to read the next step.

"You are about to embark on the most glorious

adventure in the history of time," I read out loud. "You alone will fly with the falcons. You alone will sail toward the sun. Are you ready?"

I nodded yes.

"You say, yes?"

I nodded yes again.

"You are wrong. You are not ready. Turn the page."

I turned the page — to the last page in the book.

"Empty one quarter of contents of envelope into bowl. Mix well."

Envelope! What envelope?

The rest of the page was blank — except for a tiny spot of dried glue.

I ran my finger over the glue spot. That's where the envelope had been.

But where was it now?

I shook the book frantically.

Nothing fell out.

"Oh, no," I groaned. "No envelope . . . no envelope . . ."

Wait! I know!

I ran over to the trash can.

There it was!

A small black envelope. It must have fallen out when I tossed the book into the trash.

I opened it up. Measured one quarter of the bright blue powder inside — and dropped it into the bowl.

I mixed well.

The yellow blob of dough turned green. Then it began to grow and bubble. Small bubbles at first — popping lightly on the surface. Then larger ones — growing from deep inside the dough. Rising to the surface. Bursting open with a loud PLOP.

PLOP. PLOP. PLOP.

Yuck!

I stood back.

The dough began to throb — like a beating heart.

I watched in horror as it started to gurgle.

I gulped.

What was in that envelope? Maybe it was some kind of poison!

Forget about flying. No way am I eating this gross garbage! I decided.

No way.

10

I grabbed the sides of the bowl — to dump the mixture into the trash. But I snatched my hands back when the dough flopped over, all by itself.

It flopped again and again, each time making a sickening sucking sound.

My stomach lurched.

I reached out again — and the phone rang.

"We're on our way home, Jack." Dad was calling from the car. He sounded disappointed.

"So soon?" I asked. "What happened?"

"The band members had a big fight. They called us in the car. They said don't bother coming to Anaheim. They broke up the act." I heard Dad sigh.

"Wow, Dad. I don't know what to say."

"Not to worry, Jack. I still feel lucky. Don't know why. But I do. The BIG one is coming. I can feel it. We're on the freeway. Should be home in half an hour," he said. Then he hung up.

Ugh. I better dump this stuff before they get back, I told myself.

I turned to the kitchen table — and shrieked in horror. "Morty — no! NO! What have you done?"

11

"Morty! DOWN!" I screamed.

Morty stood on the kitchen chair.

His front paws rested on the table.

His head dipped into the mixing bowl — as he swallowed a big glob of green dough.

"NO, Morty! DOWN!" I screamed again.

Morty lifted his head.

He licked his chops.

Then dove into the bowl for another bite.

I sprang across the room.

I peered down into the bowl.

"Oh, noooo!" I howled. Almost half the dough was gone!

"Morty! What did you do!" I pulled his head out of the bowl.

Morty stared up at me — his eyes wide with guilt. His ears drooped low.

He whimpered softly. Then he dipped his head back into the bowl for another bite.

I scooped him off the chair.

Carried him into the living room — and gasped as he floated up out of my hands.

I stared in disbelief as Morty floated through the room. Back into the kitchen.

"Morty — you're flying!" I cried.

It worked! I couldn't believe it! My cocker spaniel was FLYING!

I followed him — in a daze.

Followed him as he floated over the kitchen table.

Watched in amazement as he flew out the open window.

"Morty!" I cried, jolted back to reality. "Wait!"

Morty let out a sharp yelp — then sailed up, up into the sky.

I ran outside — and gazed up.

Morty soared above the house.

Floating higher and higher.

"Morty — no! Morty!" I screamed. "Morty — come back!"

His legs thrashed as he floated over the treetops. He started barking, shrill, sharp yelps of terror.

"Morty —! Morty —!"

I watched him sail up, his body rocked by the wind, his legs scrambling as if trying to grab hold of something.

"Oh, nooooo!" I wailed, staring helplessly.

I've got to get him back! I've got to rescue Morty!

But how?

12

I knew how.

I knew how to rescue my dog. And I knew I had no choice.

I ran in to the house.

I plunged my hand into the bowl. Grabbed up a big chunk of the disgusting mixture.

Yuck! I can't eat this! IT FEELS SO SLIMY!

You have to eat it, I ordered myself. You have to save Morty. It's the only way!

The dough throbbed and gurgled in my palm.

A thin mist of steam rose up from my fingers.

"Ohhh," I groaned as I shoved a fistful of the stuff into my mouth.

I clutched my throat. I started to gag.

It tasted sour and hot. It scorched my tongue.

I choked it down.

And grabbed up another glob.

Shoved it into my mouth. Swallowed hard.

My mouth and tongue swelled. Swelled with the horrible, bitter taste.

I shoved in another handful. I had to make sure I could fly like Morty.

I could feel the mixture throbbing as it slid down my throat.

Gagging, I ran back outside.

I gazed up into the sky.

Morty flew high over the trees. His cries drifted down to the ground.

I could see his legs still flailing wildly as he floated higher and higher.

He looked so small up there.

Just a dark speck in the sky now.

"I'm coming, Morty!" I cupped my hands around my mouth and yelled. "Don't worry, boy. I'll save you!"

I raised my arms up to the sky.

"I WILL FLY!" I cried out. "FLY!"

It's a bird! It's a plane!
It's a ... kid?

Goosebumps

Jack just found the coolest book. It's
called *Flying Lessons*—and it explains
how humans can learn to fly like birds!
And after doing some exercises,
repeating a chant, and drinking a
magic potion, Jack *does* learn! Finally
he's found a way to prove he's better
than his rival, Wilson! Unless Wilson
has learned to fly too....

HOW I LEARNED TO FLY
Goosebumps #52
R.L. Stine

Find it at a bookstore near you!

GBT696
© 1996 Parachute Press, Inc. GOOSEBUMPS is a registered trademark of Parachute Press, Inc. All rights reserved.

GET
Goosebumps®
by R.L. Stine

© 1996 Parachute Press, Inc. GOOSEBUMPS is a registered trademark of Parachute Press, Inc. All rights reserved.

❑ BAB93954-8	**Goosebumps Presents TV Episode #7** **My Hairiest Adventure**	$3.99
❑ BAB93955-6	**Goosebumps Presents TV Episode #8** **Be Careful What You Wish For**	$3.99
❑ BAB62836-4	**Tales to Give You Goosebumps** **Book & Light Set Special Edition #1**	$11.95
❑ BAB26603-9	**More Tales to Give You Goosebumps** **Book & Light Set Special Edition #2**	$11.95
❑ BAB74150-4	**Even More Tales to Give You Goosebumps** **Book and Boxer Shorts Pack Special Edition #3**	$14.99

―――――――――― GIVE YOURSELF GOOSEBUMPS ――――――――――

❑ BAB55323-2	**Give Yourself Goosebumps #1:** **Escape from the Carnival of Horrors**	$3.99
❑ BAB56645-8	**Give Yourself Goosebumps #2:** **Tick Tock, You're Dead**	$3.99
❑ BAB56646-6	**Give Yourself Goosebumps #3:** **Trapped in Bat Wing Hall**	$3.99
❑ BAB67318-1	**Give Yourself Goosebumps #4:** **The Deadly Experiments of Dr. Eeek**	$3.99
❑ BAB67319-X	**Give Yourself Goosebumps #5:** **Night in Werewolf Woods**	$3.99
❑ BAB67320-3	**Give Yourself Goosebumps #6:** **Beware of the Purple Peanut Butter**	$3.99
❑ BAB67321-1	**Give Yourself Goosebumps #7:** **Under the Magician's Spell**	$3.99
❑ BAB84765-1	**Give Yourself Goosebumps #8:** **The Curse of the Creeping Coffin**	$3.99
❑ BAB84766-X	**Give Yourself Goosebumps #9:** **The Knight in Screaming Armor**	$3.99
❑ BAB84767-8	**Give Yourself Goosebumps #10:** **Diary of a Mad Mummy**	$3.99
❑ BAB84768-6	**Give Yourself Goosebumps #11:** **Deep in the Jungle of Doom**	$3.99
❑ BAB84772-4	**Give Yourself Goosebumps #12:** **Welcome to the Wicked Wax Museum**	$3.99
❑ BAB84773-2	**Give Yourself Goosebumps #13:** **Scream of the Evil Genie**	$4.50

❑ BAB53770-9	**The Goosebumps Monster Blood Pack**	$11.95
❑ BAB50995-0	**The Goosebumps Monster Edition #1**	$12.95
❑ BAB93371-X	**The Goosebumps Monster Edition #2**	$12.95
❑ BAB60265-9	**Goosebumps Official Collector's Caps Collecting Kit**	$5.99
❑ BAB73906-9	**Goosebumps Postcard Book**	$7.95
❑ BAB73902-6	**The 1997 Goosebumps 365 Scare-a-Day Calendar**	$8.95
❑ BAB73907-7	**The Goosebumps 1997 Wall Calendar**	$10.99

Scare me, thrill me, mail me GOOSEBUMPS now!

Available wherever you buy books, or use this order form. Scholastic Inc., P.O. Box 7502,
2931 East McCarty Street, Jefferson City, MO 65102

Please send me the books I have checked above. I am enclosing $_____ (please add $2.00 to cover shipping and handling). Send check or money order — no cash or C.O.D.s please.

Name _____ Age _____

Address _____

City _____ State/Zip _____

Please allow four to six weeks for delivery. Offer good in the U.S. only. Sorry, mail orders are not available to residents of Canada. Prices subject to change.

R.L. STINE
GIVE YOURSELF

Goosebumps®

He warned you to stay out of the back room.
Did you listen? *Nooooo* . . .

You and your friends discover a creepy old
man inside his creepy old house. "Stay out of
my back room," he says, but you ignore his
warning—and enter anyway. You see two
huge electrical switches: One transports you
to a world of mirrors that do more than just
make you *look* strange; the other sends you
to a place where everything—and everyone—
is a robot.

Quick! Find your way back to the professor's
work room before you become a pile of nuts
and bolts! Choose from more than 20 eerie
endings!

Give Yourself Goosebumps #14
The Creepy Creations of
Professor Shock

Coming soon to a bookstore near you!

© 1996 Parachute Press, Inc. GOOSEBUMPS is a registered trademark of Parachute Press, Inc. All rights reserved.   GYGBT694

From the #1 Kids show on Fox TV!

Goosebumps®

PRESENTS

TV EPISODE #9

Todd loves worms. But after he cuts one in half, they don't love him back. Now there are worms in Todd's bed, in his spaghetti, even on his toothbrush! It seems the worms have a plan of their own . . .

Goosebumps Presents TV Episode #9

Go Eat Worms!
by R.L. Stine

WITH
8 PAGES OF
FULL-COLOR
PHOTOS FROM
THE SHOW!

Look for it in a bookstore near you!

© 1996 Parachute Press, Inc. GOOSEBUMPS is a registered trademark of Parachute Press, Inc. All rights reserved.

GBTV696

THE TERROR-ific Video Series
BASED ON YOUR FAVORITE BOOKS!

Goosebumps®

R.L. STINE
Goosebumps

A NIGHT IN TERROR TOWER

R.L. STINE
Goosebumps

STAY OUT OF THE BASEMENT

NOW ON VIDEO!

- **FREE 3-D Sticker in every video!**
- **Only $14.98 or less each!**

WATCH "GOOSEBUMPS™" EVERY WEEK ON FOX KIDS NETWORK!

20th CENTURY FOX HOME ENTERTAINMENT

PARACHUTE PRESS, INC.

SCHOLASTIC

© 1996 Parachute Press, Inc. GOOSEBUMPS is a registered trademark of Parachute Press, Inc. All rights reserved. © 1996 Twentieth Century Fox Home Entertainment, Inc. All rights reserved. "Twentieth Century Fox," "Fox," and their associated logos are the property of Twentieth Century Fox Film Corporation.